ELIZABETH JOHNS

A SERIES OF ELEMENTS BOOK TWO

Cover Design by Wilette Youkey

Edited by Tessa Shapcott and Heather King

ISBN-13: 978- 0-9965754-3-0

ISBN-10: 0-9965754-3-X

To my sisters

ELIZABETH JOHNS

A SERIES OF ELEMENTS BOOK TWO

Prologue

"This is the first time we will be apart," Beaujolais announced sadly to her triplet sisters, who were sitting with her on a large canopied bed in their London town house. They were enjoying their nightly ritual of gathering in Margaux's room. Anjou, Beaujolais and Margaux were the identical beautiful daughters of the Marquess of Ashbury and his French Marchioness.

"It is not forever, dear," Margaux said soothingly as she brushed her sister's long ebony locks to a silky sheen. "We will be together again. There will be house parties and holidays…"

"It was bound to happen sooner or later. I thought we would all be married by now. Yet, here we are, on the shelf!" Beaujolais exclaimed.

"I am happy to be claiming my space on the shelf if it means leaving the Marriage Mart! You must admit I have lost the ability to hold my tongue. It is best I leave before I ruin you all," Margaux said laughingly.

"Yes, dear, we know. But a convent? Did you truly think *Maman* would allow it?" Anjou asked sceptically as she flashed her brilliant blue eyes at her sister.

"No. At least they are allowing me to go to help with the orphanage in Scotland," Margaux replied, apparently satisfied with her lot.

"I would wager *Maman* will have you back here in less than three months," Anjou taunted while she mindlessly twisted her hair about her finger.

"I accept." Margaux held out her hand to shake on it, never one to shun sisterly competition.

"Stop, you two," Beaujolais said with disgust. "Could you not be happy here? Could you not beg *Maman* to simply let you stay at home?"

Margaux shook her head. "As if our *maman*, grandest hostess in the kingdom, would allow her single daughter to waste away at home. But even so, it would not be enough. I want freedom, dear. Can you try to understand?"

Tears welled up in Beaujolais' eyes, causing their violet hue to deepen. "I'm sorry, Marg. I will try to be happy for you, but I cannot understand it."

Margaux sighed. "You are the one born to be a duchess, Jolie. I will leave brilliant marriages to the two of you."

"Do not tease me about being a duchess. Besides, there are only two unmarried dukes in the kingdom. One is ancient and the other a recluse."

"Afraid we will curse you?" Anjou joined in taunting with her other sister. Since they were small, it had long been a source of amusement to tease Beaujolais. She had pretended to be a duchess when they had played as children, and acted the most like one. It had not helped that their mother had encouraged it.

"You *have* already turned down at least a baronet, a mister, two earls, and a marquess," Margaux pointed out helpfully.

"None could be taken seriously! And both of you have had as many offers as I," Beaujolais insisted in her own defence.

"*I* have not," Anjou boasted.

"And neither of us professes to be open to *marriage de convenance*," Margaux added.

"That is because you do not allow anyone to propose to you,"

6

Beaujolais retorted.

"I cannot consider anyone else," Anjou said looking away.

Margaux took her hand to comfort her. "It has been years without word of Aidan, Anj. Do you not think it is time to forget him?" she asked kindly.

Anjou shook her head and allowed her tears to spill down her face. "I need to do something. I cannot wait much longer for Father's enquiries." She stepped down from the bed and began to pace as she wiped her tears away. Her love, Aidan, had gone off to the American war and had not been heard from since the hostilities had ended.

"What do you propose to do?" Jolie asked with a frown.

"I want to go and look for him."

"Go and look for him?" Her sisters spoke simultaneously in disbelief.

Anjou nodded. "Charles has agreed to help me." Their brother, Charles, and Aidan had been best friends.

"*Maman* and *Papa* will never agree to that."

"They have and they will," Anjou answered quietly without looking at her sisters. "As soon as Father's enquiries are complete."

Beaujolais cried in earnest then. "It truly is the last time we will all be together!"

None of the sisters argued, but enveloped one another in a hug, wondering how life would change without the other parts of themselves.

Chapter One

"What man wants to marry unless he needs an heir?" Benedict asked scathingly.

"There are those who find companionship, if not love, with a lady, your Grace," Hughes remarked encouragingly, with little regard for his Grace's tone.

"Ladies are good for one thing only," Benedict retorted.

"But you must marry one of them to produce a legitimate heir."

"Must I?" he asked softly with an underlying challenge in his voice.

"The last heir has died, your Grace."

"You are certain?" he questioned, though he knew the answer Hughes would give him.

"Quite, quite certain. Mr Norton has made an exhaustive search." The secretary held up the damning news just received from the solicitor.

"I see."

"It must be done, your Grace."

Benedict Stanton, Duke of Yardley, sighed loudly. He was now faced with the one thing he had vowed never to do again: marry. He remained silent, digesting this new-found information along with his beefsteak and kidney pie, which was suddenly souring his stomach.

The Duke's secretary was used to his Grace's ways, and stood quietly while his employer made a decision.

Benedict exhaled audibly again.

"I suppose, Hughes, that you have made me a list?"

"Yes, your Grace." The ever-efficient secretary promptly produced a list with twelve names and their résumés, including bloodlines,

8

properties and dowries.

"As you can see, your Grace, I have listed them in order of eligibility."
He paused.

Benedict shooed the list away.

"You may begin negotiations with the first one on the list. I have little
care for their qualities other than breeding."

The secretary cleared his throat nervously, which produced an elevated
eyebrow from his Grace.

"I also took the liberty of providing those considered to be
Incomparables."

The secretary placed the list on the desk before the Duke.

"Incomparable is synonymous with idiot, Hughes. Is there a point?"

"Perhaps not quite synonymous, your Grace. Let me tactfully say that
some of the Eligibles are not necessarily of prime stock, whereas
others…" he said in a coaxing tone, using horseflesh terminology most
likely to convince the Duke, who preferred equine company to human.

"I care little for appearances," the Duke snapped.

"I think it best for you to make the decision, your Grace. Or I could
ask the Duchess…"

His Grace ignored the last taunt about involving his mother. "I should
send you to negotiations with…" he glanced at the first name on the list.
"…Cohen's daughter, a Lady Mary. But I gather you do not approve?"

"Lady Mary is all that is amiable, your Grace, but she resembles your
finest Arabians and she titters."

The Duke cringed. Perhaps a mite of scrutiny would be called for.

"Have you seen all of them?"

The secretary flushed red. "Certainly, your Grace."

Yardley stared in stupefaction at the sight of his normally staid secretary, who was blushing like a fresh youth.

"Very well. Make an offer to the first one you deem most suitable to my preferences."

The secretary bowed and left the room.

Benedict wanted little to do with any female ever again, unless they had four legs. It had been nearly ten years since his first fiasco of a marriage, and the taste in his mouth was as bitter now as the day it had happened.

He stood, tossing his napkin on the table, and walked over to look out of the window. The only reason he had gone to London during the past decade was to vote in Parliament on something his conscience would not allow him to ignore.

"I suppose I must go to London," he said to himself begrudgingly.

Must go to London. He closed his eyes in pain. Could he do it? He had not been into Society since Lillian. The scandal had been long ago, but there would always be whispers. He had little doubt it would present a problem when it came to a marriage agreement, but dealing with the looks and whispers did not interest him. Society had proven itself partially liable for his first nuptial failure, and he did not intend to allow it to happen again. Could he avoid London and negotiate through the post? Rather a shabby way of doing business, but he could not bring himself to woo anyone properly with false sentiment.

He had told his lifelong friend, Lord Easton, he would bring his prized mare for breeding with one of Easton's stallions. His family seat was in Sussex, not so far from London. Perhaps he could avoid Society as much as possible if a marriage could be arranged beforehand. He should mention to Hughes about finding someone who did not expect to live in London or care much for Society. Certainly Hughes was astute enough to know such a thing.

If Benedict was feeling sufficiently generous, he might even pay his mother and sister a visit. His mother preferred to live at the Langdon estate on the coast near Brighton when she was not in London, which suited Benedict just fine. He adored her, but they could not bring themselves to agree on certain matters—mainly his remarrying—and it was more peaceful to live in separate abodes.

He went to his desk to pen a note to his mother, and another to Lord Easton, before ringing for his valet to instruct him to pack for the trip.

Jolie pulled her horse to a halt as she skirted the edge of the chalk cliffs, inhaling the scent of the sea. As fond as she was of London, this reprieve to her cousin, Lord Easton's, estate had been welcome. This Season did not boast any new suitors she could take seriously, and her family had all departed England, leaving her feeling lonely for the first time that she could remember.

She would return to London soon, with Lady Easton as her chaperone, but there was not one serious contender for her affections. She would never confess to anyone, save her sisters, her fears of becoming a spinster. Her sister, Margaux, would rather that than marry someone she could not love. But not Jolie. She wished for a good match with someone she could respect, and who could make her life comfortable. She was not so mercenary as to accept anyone. She had, in fact, turned down so many proposals she had been teasingly nicknamed Ice, though nothing could be less apt to describe her. She had simply never found said qualities in one person. She did not require a title, contrary to popular belief, though being a duchess certainly would not hurt, she thought disdainfully to herself.

She urged her horse onwards again and enjoyed an exhilarating gallop across the Downs, while the wind whipped at her with all its might. Her cousin owned famous breeding stables, and she was enjoying the fruits of them immensely. Riding—no, galloping—was the one thing she missed the most when in town.

As she entered the house, stripping off her riding gloves and handing her crop to the butler, she was informed that her father's man of business awaited her company in the library.

"Thank you, Barnes." She smiled charmingly at the elderly earl's butler who had served her uncle Wyndham since before she was born. Why would her father's solicitor be seeking her out? It was Anjou who was awaiting news. Perhaps there was news of Aidan, and just after Anjou had set out! She tidied her wind-blown hair as much as she could. She entered through the doorway to find her cousin, Mr Harlow, and another man in deep conversation. She paused and knocked.

"Ah, Jolie. Please join us," Lord Easton said as all of the men stood.

"Lady Beaujolais, may I present Mr Norton, and you are acquainted with Mr Harlow, I believe."

She nodded as the men bowed. She took her seat and looked curiously to her cousin.

"Jolie, Mr Norton is here on behalf of the Duke of Yardley."

What has that to do with me? She wondered, but kept her tongue. Her pulse sped up nevertheless. She had heard of Yardley, the Duke who was reputed to be cold and reclusive, but had never met him herself.

"I will let you explain, Mr Norton, if you would," her cousin said.

"Your ladyship, I will be brief. His Grace has decided to marry, and has selected you as his choice."

An unaccountable wave of anger swept through her. Was the Duke sending his proposal of marriage through his solicitor without so much as an introduction? How dared he! He felt himself to be above common civilities? True, it was flattering in some respects, but she would never marry someone so arrogant, so…so…she could not even think of a proper word to describe his audacity! Had he made an arrangement with her father to pay his addresses? No, her father would never do such. She sat in silence, attempting to control her temper and manage a dignified response. All that came from her mouth was, "I see."

The solicitor must have interpreted her silence as shocked pleasure, for he continued. "He has made you a most generous settlement, my lady."

He handed her a piece of paper outlining his offer. She struggled to keep the paper from shaking in her hands.

"You will be settled in high style, with your own house and estate and several thousand pounds a year. And it is not contingent on providing an heir," the solicitor said, as if she should be flattered.

Jolie could feel her cousin's eyes on her. She met them with her own questioningly, and could see by his expression that he was as shocked as she was. How would her father have handled this? She supposed Easton felt it was her decision to make. She had to take a deep breath so she did not strangle the messenger. She stood and waved the men back to their seats while she walked to the window, her thoughts in a whirl.

After a few moments she turned and asked, "Sir, would you be so good as to inform his Grace that I would rather rot in hell than accept his offer."

She tore the settlement in two and dropped it in his lap.

"Gentlemen," she said as she walked out of the room.

Chapter Two

Jolie walked from the study out to the garden. Feeding the birds was a daily pleasure for her. Even in town she made time for it. She took a handful of crumbs and sat on a bench, and the birds began to pick at the food as she tossed it onto the path.

Her cousin Easton followed her outside and leaned against the nearby balustrade.

"Forgive me if I was rude. Do I overreact?" Jolie asked her cousin without looking up.

Easton pondered a moment before answering.

"No. If he had been requesting permission to pay his addresses to you, perhaps. But a marriage proposal through the solicitor is rather antiquated and in poor taste, even if he is a duke."

Jolie let out a satisfied *harrumph*. She had been feeling ashamed of her dramatic refusal in front of the two solicitors. It had not been well done of her.

"The thing is, I have known Yardley since Eton and I am astonished," Easton remarked.

"You know the reclusive Duke?" Jolie looked up at her cousin without masking the awe in her voice.

Easton smiled. "Intimately."

Jolie was impressed despite herself. "Is it true about him, then? I confess to know little of him other than tidbits I overheard about a divorce and a duel. I was rather young, and *Maman* would not tell me all. He is scarcely referred to in town except as the reclusive Duke."

"How often are rumours true?" Easton answered with a question.

"There is often some truth in them," she countered.

"He is divorced, but the wife died. All is not as Society has portrayed it to be."

"Did I make a mistake?" Jolie's spirits sank.

"No. Would you be happy in such a relationship?" He held up his hands. "Despite your protests?"

Jolie thought a few moments before answering. "No, perhaps not. But I also never imagined myself for a love match."

Easton chuckled. "Of all three sisters, you are the one I think most suited for a love match. If you could but observe yourself with the animals, and see your tender heart, you might think differently."

"I suppose," she said doubtfully. "I had always assumed to make a good marriage and have respect for my husband. I think that is enough for me."

"Do you not consider Yardley a suitable match?" Easton asked with raised eyebrows. "It would be difficult to contemplate a more brilliant position in Society."

"You surprise me, Cousin. You of all people care nothing for position and society. I have not even met the man."

"Quite true. However, your father is not here and I am doing my best at wise counsel."

She laughed. "Very well. My sisters would not credit that I have refused a duke."

"As much as I am certain you have been teased, I think you realise yourself worthy of a modicum of respect. Even the title of Duchess would not be worth demeaning yourself for."

"Thank you, Easton," Jolie remarked softly, grateful that her cousin supported her.

"You should, perhaps, be open-minded. If Yardley needs a wife, he is bound to make an appearance before long. If Yardley wants you, make him come to ask you."

"He has likely already sent his solicitor to the next fortunate lady on the list."

"He might have done. But I do think you should prepare yourself for meeting him. Maybe it will alter your opinion."

"Never."

Jolie excused herself to go and change out of her riding habit. Easton stood watching the Channel in the distance, pondering how to handle this unexpected development, and if he should involve himself on either his friend or his cousin's behalf. He was responsible for Jolie while her parents were in Scotland.

"Is something on your mind, my love?" Lady Easton, Elly to her intimates, asked as she joined her husband, leaning her arms on the balustrade.

Easton smiled at her and bent over to kiss her head. "I'm pondering whether or not to tell Jolie that Yardley is to visit."

"Because he is a duke?" Elly asked with a mischievous grin. She was aware of Jolie's purported desire to be a duchess.

"Yes and no." Easton told Elly how Yardley had sent a marriage proposal through his solicitor.

"Are they not acquainted at all?"

"No. Jolie only knows Yardley by reputation. I have no idea what compelled him to offer for her."

"I cannot believe it of him," Elly said with a wrinkled brow.

"I confess myself also surprised. However, you are one of the few females he can tolerate. He is not himself any more in Society since his first marriage."

"Is that the reason he sent his solicitor? I cannot credit that behaviour from what I know of him. I would have thought he and Jolie well suited."

"He is still bitter and has a very low opinion of most females."

"But Jolie is a superb rider and loves animals. Not to mention her beauty. He could not help but love her. If he took the time to know her, of course."

"I wonder why he chose Jolie. In fact, I wonder what made him decide to remarry at all. It is out of character for him." Easton shook his head. "No matter. He will be here and can answer those questions soon. Should I request he stay with his mother? Her estate is not over far."

"Let me think on it," Elly said. "I wish to speak with Jolie about it first. I have an idea, however."

"Should I be afraid?" Easton teased.

"Of course not!" Elly elbowed him playfully in the arm as she would her brother. "I will inform you as soon as I see how upset she is and decide how best to handle the situation."

"Very well. Benedict is one of my oldest friends, and I would like to see him happy again. Playing match-maker is another thing altogether."

"We shall not match-make. We shall merely provide opportunity."

Easton shook his head. "I am certain I shall regret this."

Elly replied with a laugh.

~*~

Dinner was a smaller affair than usual, with the old Earl taking his meal in his rooms and with the departure of the rest of the Ashbury family. The only dinner guests were Lady Easton's brother, Andrew, and his wife, Gwen, who were not considered guests since they now lived on

17

the property. Several years prior, Lord Easton had opened a school to train orphans in medicine, and his cousin, Nathaniel, Lord Fairmont, had added a veteran's home after Waterloo. Fairmont had lost an eye and an arm in the harrowing battle.

They also bred and raised horses on the estate, and it had become a family affair for the Loring, Abbott, and Trowbridge families.

Gwen was expecting another blessed event in the next month, and she preferred Elly be with her for her confinement since she had medical expertise, in addition to being her sister-in-law.

Therefore, Jolie's return to London would be delayed. With dinner being an intimate family affair, none felt obliged to mind their tongues, especially Elly and Andrew, who considered roasting one another with wit to be a virtue.

"I hope you do not mind horribly having to wait to return to London," Gwen said to Jolie. "I assure you, I am as ready as you for little Abbott to introduce himself to the world."

"I do not mind," Jolie reassured her. "I am rather enjoying this reprieve. I am not certain how entertaining the Season will be without my sisters."

"Ah. You will have to experience *ton* life as a mere singleton," Andrew jested. "It is not as easy when you've no one to hide behind."

"And how would you know this? It is hardly the same for males as for females. We are expected to remain passively on the side until we are asked to dance. I beg you to recall one time you were obliged to hide," Elly insisted.

"I can think of any number of times I was obliged to hide from mamas on the hunt, or from Grandmama. Mostly from Gran," Andrew said with a grin.

"You have no one you are impatient to return to, then?" Gwen asked politely.

Jolie, Easton, and Elly all looked up at the same time. Andrew did not miss the look that passed between them.

"You might as well tell us," Andrew remarked. "It will out sooner or later."

"I am sorry if I chose a poor subject," Gwen said apologetically. "I assumed Jolie would not be lacking for suitors."

"Only silly or insufferable ones," Jolie muttered.

"Methinks curiosity needs satisfaction," Andrew said with interest.

"Jolie had an offer today from Yardley," Easton said.

Andrew looked surprised.

"Not from Yardley, precisely—his solicitor," Elly explained.

"When is the wedding?" Andrew smiled.

"Andrew! Jolie has never so much as set on eyes on the Duke," Elly chastised her brother.

"What has that to do with anything? She wants to be a duchess, he is a duke, he made an offer. It has worked that way for centuries. There are not too many dukes to choose from, at all events. Besides, we can muster an introduction. I say, is he not…"

Andrew felt a kick in the shin from his sister and she shook her head.

"Is he not…charming?" Andrew asked awkwardly, wondering why Elly did not want him to mention Yardley's visit.

"I do not wish for an introduction, Andrew, regardless of my inclination to be a duchess." Jolie made a self-deprecating face. "I would prefer a husband who would communicate in person."

"You might not," Elly teased, with a wink towards her husband.

"Does this mean Yardley is coming out from seclusion?" Andrew asked.

"He has not informed me of his intentions. I am as astonished as the rest of you by his offer. I would not say he has been in seclusion, but he has certainly not been into Society."

"I will attempt to be civil if we are introduced. I do not wish to make you uncomfortable around your friend," Jolie added graciously.

"No danger of that. In fact, you are welcome to tell him exactly what you thought of his offer," Easton said with an amused smile.

"Make sure I am there to watch," Andrew requested.

Elly sent her brother an exasperated glance, placed her napkin on the table and stood. "Shall we, ladies?"

The ladies removed to the drawing room and made themselves comfortable for a tête-à-tête while they awaited the men.

"May I be bold, Jolie?" Elly asked in her usually frank fashion.

"Of course," Jolie reassured her.

"Why did you refuse Yardley outright? You could have negotiated an introduction."

Jolie looked down at her hands. "I suppose so, but it infuriated me. I know it seems silly, but it felt wrong."

"I do not think it silly at all," Gwen said. "I always go with my instinct."

Jolie smiled at her.

"Have you heard so many rumours in town?" Elly asked.

"I confess, it may be part of my reaction. He is said to be cold-hearted, and to have treated his first wife very ill."

Gwen let out a sympathetic gasp. Elly sat thoughtfully for a moment.

"It is even said that he killed a man in a duel, though of course one does not know of these things."

"I only ask one thing." Elly took Jolie's hand and gave it a squeeze. "Judge him for yourself if you do meet him, do not base your opinion on rumour. It is what you would wish for yourself."

~*~

Benedict rode his mare through the gates leading to his mother's estate, situated high above the Channel. He had attempted to prepare himself for her and his sister, but he abandoned it somewhere shortly after turning south from Yardley. His mind had been distracted by the impending leg-shackles he was about to acquire, and the fact that news from his solicitor regarding the settlements would be awaiting him. He was looking forward to visiting his friend Easton, if nothing else excited him about this trip.

He had elected to travel alone, having sent his baggage and valet on ahead. He could never abide a carriage if he had the choice of riding. Horses had saved him after his marriage ended in disaster, and he infinitely preferred them to humans. Benedict laughed when he saw his mother exit through the front door and wave furiously at him with uncharacteristic exuberance. She was an unlikely duchess, being a bit peculiar and languid, but she was a duchess, nonetheless. Benedict never failed to feel guilty for his introversion when he knew how much his mother enjoyed his presence.

He reined in his mount before tossing the reins to the waiting groom.

"Mother," Benedict said, as he kissed his mother's offered hand.

She took a deep breath and smiled at him. "Now I can be happy again."

"You are always happy, dearest," he reassured her as she took his arm and began to walk into the house.

"It is my duty to be so. However, it is not the same when you are

21

away. Off in that horrid, cold house all alone."

"I am hardly alone, Mother."

"I do not know where that sister of yours is," the Duchess muttered and looked around. "Likely off with her nose in a book."

"There is little enough harm in that. I will see her at dinner," he said, unconcerned.

"She is more interested in her books than suitors. Perhaps you can talk her into going to London. She refused to be brought out this year," the Duchess explained, as though he were unaware of the fact from her weekly letters.

"I am beginning to think my sister has more sense than I gave her credit for," he remarked.

"Do not side with her! She is to turn eighteen this summer," his mother opined.

"Hello, Walters," Benedict said as he handed the butler his hat and coat.

"Welcome, your Grace. Mr Norton is here and has been for some time. I took the liberty of placing him in the study with a luncheon tray."

"I did forget about him. I wish you would not hide in there all day on business when I have not seen you this age!" his mother said despondently.

"I do think this is business of which you will approve," he replied obscurely.

Benedict turned towards the study as his mother remonstrated. "It is ill-mannered to tease!" But she would pry no more from him.

He chuckled and walked into the study, in surprisingly good humour knowing the fate awaiting him inside.

"Your Grace!" Mr Norton jumped from the armchair in which he was resting.

"Do sit, Mr Norton. I assume you have news?"

The man was fidgeting nervously and Benedict had little tolerance for diffidence.

"Get on with it, sir. I will not bite," Benedict urged impatiently.

"Very well. The lady refused your offer, your Grace," the solicitor exhaled as if he felt liberated at being relieved of a severe burden.

"I see." Benedict needed a moment to absorb this unexpected turn of events. When he looked up, the solicitor was fidgeting again. "Is there something else you wish to say?"

"I do not precisely *wish* to say it, your Grace. But the lady did have a message for you."

Benedict raised his eyebrows. "And what message was this?"

"That she would rather rot in hell than accept your offer," the solicitor mumbled.

"And may I ask who this well-spoken lady was?" he asked mockingly.

"Lord Ashbury's daughter, your Grace. Shall I move on to another name on the list?"

"Did she say precisely why?" Benedict was unfathomably interested.

"She did not happen to mention it," the solicitor answered.

"That will be all for now, Mr Norton. I will let you know if I wish to proceed."

A look of surprise passed on the solicitor's face before he bowed and let himself from the room.

Benedict sat staring out of the window for some time, pondering his next course of action.

Chapter Three

"Good morning," Jolie greeted her cousins as they entered the breakfast room after they had finished their morning walk with the children.

"You are an early riser today," Easton remarked.

"I want to see the cliffs in the early sun. Would you mind if I borrow one of your riding habits, Elly? I seem to have torn the hem on mine and I did not bring a spare."

"Certainly. You may borrow anything you wish," Elly said as she buttered a slice of toast.

"I confess, I have been longing to try one of your split-legged skirts," Jolie admitted.

"You will never want to ride side-saddle again if you try it," Elly said, grinning.

"You could try out Hector if you are going to ride astride," Easton offered.

"Oh, Adam! You are the best of all cousins," Jolie exclaimed.

"You can handle him, but you must take a groom. I have a friend bringing a mare to be put to Hector as stud, and he could use a good ride before she arrives." He chuckled.

"I will take him through his paces then," she said as she hurried out of the room.

When she was gone, Easton spoke with Elly about their discussion from the previous day.

"Are you going to tell me what your plans are for Yardley and Jolie? He sent word he would be here today."

"So soon?" Elly looked up from her coffee. "Will he be staying here, this time?"

"He is staying with his mother and sister near Rottingdean. It is not above eight miles," Easton remarked.

"I have not yet decided how best to handle the situation. I believe if they had the opportunity to know one another they would find they would suit very well indeed."

"Yardley might not forgive her words if the solicitor was stupid enough to repeat them to him," Easton pointed out.

"She might not wish to know him either," Elly answered, trying hard to think of a solution.

"If only they could know one another without their titles," Easton said, jesting.

"Maybe we could make that happen."

"How? They are both too proper to speak without an introduction," he said doubtfully.

"Even if it were at the stables?"

"I do not know. It would require warning the staff," he said hesitantly. "And your brother."

"That is easily done. Yardley prefers not to be known by his title in non-public situations," she pointed out.

"But you do not think she will find it odd if I introduce her as Jolie?"

"I have confidence in you. Just say, 'This is my cousin, Jolie Winslow', and change the subject."

"And what happens if we make a mistake?" he questioned.

"We beg forgiveness for our poor manners and plead eccentricity."

Easton sighed and shook his head. "I have not had the benefit of living in America as an excuse." He then changed the subject before his wife could retort, though she balled up her napkin and tossed it at him. "Father said Livvy is returning from school next week. Do you think we should take her to London with us?"

"I thought we had agreed to bring her out in the autumn?"

"I have a notion she will want to join us when she finds out you are chaperoning Jolie."

"Yes, I suppose you are right. Have you discussed it with your father?" she asked.

"No. I am afraid he will feel obliged to accompany us. And he is not strong enough."

"Then I think you should point that out to her. But we must consider Livvy might have to delay her coming out for mourning," she said gently.

"Yes, I fear you are correct. We had so many more years than we expected, thanks to you."

She reached across and held his hand. "Let us pray we have many more."

~*~

Benedict rode along the path beside the sea between Rottingdean and the Wyndham estate near Seaford. It was a beautiful late spring morning, and he enjoyed the sun shining on his face and the wind whipping against him. The feeling of speed and freedom never failed to produce a surge of excitement in him that made any problem seem minuscule.

He had slept on his marital dilemma, and decided to seek advice from his oldest friend. Easton would guide him in the right direction. It had been far too long since he had confided in anyone other than himself.

He spied another rider in the distance, and the vision was enough to force him to concentrate to keep his seat, in addition to controlling his mare. He pulled off the path to admire the view. He did not know what to make of the entire scene: a petite female riding all out on a giant beast of a horse. She was sitting atop its back astride and had wild black hair whipping beneath her beaver. She continued straight towards him, tipping her hat and smiling brilliantly as she passed.

Benedict was still assimilating his thoughts a few minutes later when a groom passed, attempting to catch his mistress. *No chance of that*, he thought. By the time he rode into the Wyndham estate, he had almost convinced himself he had dreamt the girl in his mind. He went straight to the stables, suspecting he would find his friend there, as usual. He was all anticipation to see the stallion Easton had been telling him about.

"Benny!" Easton exclaimed, using his childhood nickname, and went to greet him. He and Andrew had been breaking a horse and were in their shirtsleeves and muddy boots. The head groom took the reins from Andrew.

"Easton, Abbott." He greeted both men with equal pleasure.

"Where is this stallion I have been dreaming about?" Benedict asked, looking around.

"I am afraid my cousin took him out for a ride. I did not know what time you would arrive, and I want Hector to be on his best behaviour when he meets your mare. Is this the beauty herself?" Easton reached out to greet the white horse, and she nickered and thrust her nose into his chest.

"Yes, this is Dido," Benedict said as he dismounted and they led her to a stall for some hay and a rub down.

"She is everything I hoped she would be. I do not see how Hector will be able to resist," Easton said cheerfully.

"Would you care to go and refresh yourself?" Andrew asked.

Benedict looked at the other men and laughed. "No, I believe I will join you. I could use some hard work and advice."

"Advice? It must be serious," Easton probed.

"I wish it were not," Benedict said remorsefully.

"Would you prefer to go back to the house?" Easton looked concerned.

"No. I am certain I will think better out here."

"Very well. We are breaking in a youngster. We could use extra hands," Easton admitted.

"He is timid with us. Perhaps he will take to you," Andrew remarked.

The men went back to the paddock, which was situated across from the stables on the opposite side of the carriage drive. A great oak tree guarded the gateway and a fence of wooden posts and rails extended along the curve of the drive to join a hawthorn hedge covered in sweet-smelling white flowers. The hedge enclosed the pasture, meeting the oak on the other side. Swathes of Queen Anne's lace and buttercups decorated the underside of the hedge.

A groom was attempting to lead the young horse by his bridle, but each time the man walked forward, taking a gentle pressure on the bit, the colt threw his head up and reared. Another groom, holding a long rope attached to the horse's cavesson and standing in the centre of a circle, flicked a long-lashed whip towards it. The colt, a handsome chestnut, bucked and plunged, almost lifting his handler–a muscled man of above-average height–off his feet. The whites of the horse's eyes showed as he swung towards the gate and the groom cursed, his boots slipping in a patch of mud worn by trampling hooves.

"He is skittish. I have never met a horse that was afraid of you. Has Elly tried to lead him?" Benedict questioned.

"Not yet. That is my next plan, but I am not ready to concede defeat."

"And the usual treats do not tempt him?" Benedict asked as he observed the horse shaking his head to evade the bridle.

"Not enough for him to come willingly."

"We rescued him from the slaughter-house. I have no idea what he endured before we found him. I will win him over eventually," Easton said as he watched the grooms continue their struggle to persuade the colt to walk quietly on the lunge.

"Does he lead in a halter or the cavesson on its own?" Benedict asked.

"As a rule, yes."

"You may have to go back a step or two, then and regain his confidence." After a short pause, he suggested. "Let him loose, while we stand away and see if he will relax."

"It is worth a try. We are getting nowhere this way," Andrew agreed, signalling to the servants to release the horse.

Andrew and Easton joined Benedict in leaning on the fence. The grooms efficiently removed the colt's harness, released him and walked away.

"I suppose now is as good a time as any to seek the advice I need," Benedict said reluctantly.

"I confess myself intrigued," Easton admitted, while Andrew remained silent and watched the horse.

"I need to remarry," he confessed.

"I gather the last cousin thirty times removed has died?" Easton asked sardonically.

"Precisely."

"That is dire, indeed," Andrew agreed.

"The two of you may jest, but neither of you was married to Lilith, *nee* Lillian."

29

"True, we both have fortunate marriages."

"Do you have any advice on how to go about finding someone?"

"The manner in which one acquires a wife has not changed."

"I must have forgotten. I offered for someone and she refused me. And she refused me rather vehemently."

Easton raised his brows. "Vehemently?"

"She told my solicitor she would rather rot in hell than accept my offer."

Andrew made a choking noise. Easton cleared his throat.

"And did this lady give signs she welcomed your suit?"

"I have never met her," Benedict confessed.

Easton and Andrew were silent.

"Tell me," Benedict demanded. "I can see you wish to say something."

"Why did you offer for someone you had not been introduced to?" Easton enquired.

Benedict let out a sigh of exasperation. "Deuce take it, you know why! I want nothing to do with marriage. It matters little who the lady is, as long as she is of good pedigree. I do not wish for an attachment. Of any sort." He clarified, "It has been done in such a manner for ages!"

"Might I suggest you make the offer in person, *after* an introduction."

Benedict ran his hands through his hair. "I suppose I must. I never anticipated my suit would be rejected. That is abominably arrogant, I know."

"That is understandable, I am sure," Andrew said with sarcasm.

"May I ask how you selected your proposed bride?" Easton lifted an enquiring eyebrow.

"Hughes did, naturally. He made me a list, and I told him to use his discretion."

Easton and Andrew exchanged glances. "You know nothing of any of the ladies on the list?"

Benedict shook his head. "Only that the first one on the list resembled an Arabian and tittered."

"Lady Mary." Andrew said with recognition. "I trust she is not the one you made the offer to?" he reasoned.

"No, but I suppose I cannot rule her out. I am tempted to know the one I made the offer to. There is something that makes me want to prove myself, however ludicrous it sounds. My pride wishes to prove her wrong."

"And what would you do if you convinced her? Do you intend to make her regret her decision?"

He shrugged his shoulders in a very ungentlemanly manner. This was one of the few places he could shed his ducal mask.

"Do you even know her name?"

He shook his head.

"I believe Hughes said it was Ashbury's daughter. I am not acquainted with Ashbury, though Hughes assures me his reputation is impeccable." The whole scenario sounded distasteful when he had to explain it to someone else. He felt irritated and disgusted with himself. He was unaccustomed to questioning his decisions.

"I realise you do not wish to enter into a love match, but it would behove you to spend a little time courting. I will likely be taking Olivia back to town with us, so I will be there to suffer with you, should you wish to go along."

"Charlotte also needs to be brought out. But I do not know if I can do it again. What if this girl refused me for my reputation? It will not be any better when the rumours start again."

"I think you make more of it than exists. Your seclusion only feeds the rumours."

"People overlook much for dukes," Andrew remarked.

"Not that there is anything to overlook. The fault was not yours," Easton reasoned.

Benedict gave a short laugh, and removing his coat and waistcoat, rolled back his sleeves. "I suppose there is no other solution."

He pulled some carrots from his pocket, which he had left from the journey. He attempted to approach the colt, his hand held out with the sweet offering. The young horse was even more terrified of a stranger. He kicked up his heels and cavorted around the paddock before careering straight at the gate. His hindquarters skidded in the muddy patch and sprayed Benedict as he stepped hastily back. Cold, wet earth splattered Benedict's face and down his front. What a way to have to make his bow to Elly!

Guffaws filled his ears. Pulling a handkerchief from his pocket and wiping the mud from his eyes, he saw Easton and Andrew laughing uproariously. Being accustomed to seeing him in a pristine condition, they would, no doubt, extract a great deal of enjoyment from the situation and all at his expense.

He could do little but laugh himself at the absurd picture he knew he must present. He walked his indignity back over to the railing.

"Very well," he held up his hands. "I have lost my touch."

"So have we, my friend. So have we."

"Perhaps we should ask Elly to help. She does have a way with them," Andrew suggested.

Easton sighed, "I suppose we must."

The men turned to the sound of hooves beating against the turf and saw Jolie riding up on Hector.

"Beautiful," Benedict said under his breath.

"The horse, or my cousin?" Easton teased him.

Benedict did not respond. He was too enthralled, staring at the picture of beauty created by the horse and his rider.

Andrew went over to help Jolie dismount. She smiled, and Benedict could not force his gaze from her. She handed the reins to Andrew and dusted herself off. She walked toward the rail, and the skittish colt ran straight toward her. Benedict lurched forward, thinking he must save her, but the colt showed no signs of hurting her. Instead, he began prancing playfully and began to nuzzle her for attention.

"Greetings, handsome. Have these men not been treating you properly?" she asked as she began to stroke his neck affectionately. The men watched with open admiration.

Benedict took the opportunity to observe her while she doted on the horse. She was not dressed like a lady and she certainly did not ride like one. Perhaps she was a poor relation. But she had a way with animals. Her brilliant violet eyes caught him staring and he almost blushed. He was beyond blushes, but he certainly was intrigued. He looked away, furious with himself for being attracted to this female. The last time he had allowed that to happen he had been humiliated. He looked to Easton curiously.

"May I present my cousin, Jolie Winslow? Jolie, this is my old school friend, Benedict Stanton," Easton said casually.

Jolie dropped a small curtsy. Benedict gave a curt nod as their eyes met. *She must not be worthy of my attention or Easton would have introduced me by my title*, he thought with a twinge of regret, although they had on occasion omitted their titles to avoid match-making.

33

He had difficulty pulling his eyes from her, yet he could not continue to stare at her without speaking. He gave another brief nod, and he turned to Easton. "May I have the pleasure of meeting Hector?"

Easton was trying not to laugh for some reason. "Certainly," he replied and addressed Jolie. "I trust he will be well behaved."

"I certainly did my best to tire him," Jolie replied.

~*~

Jolie had wanted to burst out laughing. Mr Stanton had attempted to appear dignified, but he was so endearingly covered in mud from head to toe, that she had barely been able to discern his amber eyes. She was uncertain if he was staring at her own state of *dishabille,* or if he was unaccustomed to women. One could not accuse him of being verbose. Perhaps that was why he bred horses, she reflected. Despite his dirt, he was undoubtedly handsome. He was likely a second son, not looking for marriage, and unable to support a wife in the manner in which she was accustomed. She found herself pondering whether she could she enjoy a simpler life without town. She did love town, but she did also enjoy the country.

She turned when she heard Elly and the children. They were running excitedly towards the stables for their exercise.

"Cousin Jolie!" The children exclaimed as they passed. The grooms were leading out ponies for them, and they could see the men introducing a mare to Hector.

"Let us pray Hector is well behaved," Elly commented as they observed the horses' introduction from afar.

Jolie laughed. "The children are too busy to notice either way."

Lizzie was already riding in circles around her brothers while they were mounting.

34

The children were riding away when Elly and Jolie walked to the paddock to watch the men and horses more closely.

"Did you meet Mr Stanton?" Elly asked with a twinkle in her eyes.

"I suppose one could call it an introduction. I am not certain he spoke a word."

"He is perhaps a bit reserved," Elly mused.

"Reserved? Is that it? I was not certain if he was timid or if I had shocked him. However, he was covered in mud from head to toe so he might have been conscious of the fact."

"Benedict was dirty?" Elly held up her hand to shield her gaze from the sun so she could look at the promised spectacle, and continued to walk closer to the fence. "Indeed he is! I have never before seen him with so much as a wrinkle in his neckcloth!"

Jolie watched admiringly. "He is very unlike the men in town."

"He is passionate about his horses."

"I can respect that," Jolie remarked.

"I believe Adam mentioned he is looking for a wife." Elly smiled broadly as she hinted boldly.

"Is he? He does not have that feeling about him."

"It is part of the appeal."

"Mm," Jolie sounded out distractedly as she watched him with his mare.

"It is also appealing to watch a man with his beast," Elly remarked as she looked at her husband fondly.

"Indeed," Jolie said laughing. "Very well, I confess to being intrigued."

"I do wonder if he might be persuaded to join us for tea."

"Am I to know nothing else of him?"

"It will be more amusing for you to discover things on your own," Elly teased.

"Will it?" Jolie asked doubtfully as she began to follow the other woman back to the house.

Chapter Four

Benedict had indeed been persuaded to stay for tea despite his protests, even though he had been expecting to remain, as he always did, and had brought a change of clothes. When he realised he had made a fool of himself covered in mud, as he was bathing he wished himself back in Birmingham. He was unaccountably nervous, or perhaps it was not so unaccountable. He was honest enough with himself to realise he was terrified of being near Easton's cousin. Before he had known he needed to marry, he would have dismissed her as a beauty and moved on. He wanted to do so now. But the image of her on the horse would be with him for some time, and he knew he would measure all others against that image henceforth, however unfairly.

He needed to direct Hughes to continue with the list. He could not bear to become emotionally involved again. He gave his neckcloth a final tug, and considered how he should behave towards this cousin of Easton's. He could already feel the old feelings beginning, and he had to master his self-control as he felt the silk noose begin to tighten around his neck.

By the time he had walked to the parlour, he had resolved to be indifferent and polite to the lady. How hard could it be to sit through tea? It had been too long since he had been near any unmarried women. He was out of practice. He hoped Easton and Elly would continue to refer to him as Benny and it would be easier to relax. If he could not succeed with his friends, he would never survive London.

He entered the parlour, and came face to face with pale blue muslin, wrapped around a dainty package, with a blue ribbon and matching bandeau framing her perfect face. She turned and he suddenly wished he had the dirt to hide behind again. He did, however, take a measure of gratification in the fact that her violet eyes showed a glimpse of admiration before she disguised it. They also hinted at amusement and surprise, but he would not dwell on it. He, too, admired the prospect before him. He was still uncertain of her role, be it companion or guest.

He recalled himself and bowed. "Miss Winslow."

"Mr Stanton." She curtsied.

He remained at the door with it wide open, unsure of how to proceed.

"I do believe it will be acceptable for you to join me. The others shall be down directly. Elly went to gather the children."

She sat down on a settee of puce brocade, and indicated for him to sit as well. He looked around for a place to hide, but the room was too small. He chose a chair near the mantelpiece, uncomfortable with the intimacy of a tête-à-tête. *Please let the others hurry*, he thought.

They sat in painful silence for a few moments before both spoke at the same time.

"Do you—?"

"Are you—?"

"I beg your pardon, please speak first," he indicated.

"I was making idle chit-chat." She waved her hand dismissively.

"It is a lovely day," he remarked.

She laughed and her smile was captivating. "I would not be so passé! I was going to ask where you are from."

"There you two are!" Elly exclaimed as if she had been searching for them everywhere. "Have you rung for tea? The children will be staying upstairs. They were not well behaved on their ride."

Benedict was surprised, for the children usually joined them for tea. It was one of the eccentricities of the Eastons. He did applaud discipline though, however much he wished to see them.

"I will have to come again soon if I am to be deprived of my godson."

"You know you would never be deprived. You may see him whenever you wish."

"I am delighted to hear it."

"Andrew and Gwen will not be joining us. She is feeling tired, as is normal near her time," Elly said as she took a seat.

"Is her time to be soon?" he asked politely.

"Sooner than we thought, I believe. That will please Jolie. I am certain she is bored with us in the country and is longing for town."

"I am no such thing," Jolie protested enchantingly. "I would not mind remaining here."

"No, no. I shall not keep you away once I know Gwen and the baby to be healthy," Elly said as she rang for the tea.

Easton entered the room. "I apologise if I have delayed you. I was speaking with Father."

"How is Wyndham?" Benedict asked fondly.

"Weaker every day, I am afraid. He wants us to take Olivia to London with us. He realises she should be brought out now."

"Is he strong enough for me to pay my respects before I leave?" Benedict asked, concerned.

"He would never forgive us if we forbade it!" Easton chuckled.

"Very well then. I will stop in briefly."

The butler brought in the tea tray, and Elly motioned for Jolie to do the honours.

"How did Hector take to Dido?" Elly asked as Jolie poured and handed each person their cup.

"Dido was not impressed," Benedict mused.

"Hector was tired!" Easton protested.

"Oh, dear. I did my job too well," Jolie said apologetically.

"They are only teasing. Horses have their own mating rituals. Sometimes it takes time," Elly said reassuringly.

"I confess I know little about horse-breeding," Jolie admitted.

"You know horses well, however," Benedict surprised himself by saying. "You handled the stallion with ease."

"Thank you, Mr Stanton," Jolie answered modestly.

Benedict looked up at Easton, mildly amused at being called Mr Stanton, but Elly intervened before he could comment.

"Has Charlotte gone to town yet?"

"No, apparently she prefers books to balls. My mother despairs. She thinks I might persuade her if I go. I was hoping to avoid such a fate, but it appears I must."

"Then the two of you will be together in your misery, at least," Elly said to Easton. "Let us have a small gathering for Olivia and Charlotte, since it will be the end of the Season. There will be no chance of finding an open day at this point. Only our closest friends will attend."

Benedict believed Lady Easton would be true to her word, but would his mother approve?

"It sounds agreeable to me if I am not to avoid London all together," he conceded.

He glanced at the cousin to see her reaction to his declaration, but she had her profile turned to him as she studied her teacup.

"Jolie can help me arrange the list and date from here. I will send a letter with the names to your mother for her approval."

"Certainly," Jolie agreed.

"Very well," he sighed in resignation.

"It will be better than you think, old friend," Easton said as he clapped him on the back. "Shall I take you to Father?"

~*~

Jolie watched Mr Stanton leave with her cousin, trying not to openly admire him in front of Elly. But she was enchanted. It was a new experience for her.

"That is how Benedict usually looks," Elly explained.

"He looked very gentlemanly," Jolie remarked innocently.

"I am not fooled, but you will be seeing much of him if we are to bring out Olivia and Charlotte together." Elly gave her a knowing smile.

"I will be happy to have Olivia's company. I was not looking forward to being on my own when we return. I did not expect you to spend every moment dancing attendance on me," Jolie replied evasively.

"I know, and I do not mind. I was not a Society favourite, as you are."

"If I could only do so well as you," Jolie said wistfully.

"I have little doubt, when you find the right person, you will feel compelled to accept him," Elly said with a twinkle in her eye.

"I begin to fear there is something the matter with me. I wished many times Father would arrange something for me, but he would not. Yet when I have the choice, there is no one with whom I wish to spend the rest of my life," Jolie said with mild frustration.

"You are fortunate to have the choice."

"So I am told. Little comfort does it give me now though."

Andrew flung open the door, and ran into the room, out of breath. "Elly, come!"

"What is it Andrew? Is something the matter with Gwen?" Elly asked.

"The baby!" he exclaimed by way of explanation.

"I did not expect it quite this soon." She jumped from her chair to

41

follow her brother.

"Is there anything I can do to help?" Jolie called after them. "Though I know little about childbirth."

"No, I have plenty of help with that. Make the guest list for the party," Elly suggested as Andrew was pulling her from the room.

Jolie was wishing she had paid more attention to her mother or her sister. They were good at organising, and she had learned to stay out of their household management. She supposed she could think of a guest list if she tried hard enough. She was well acquainted with the *ton*, and knew who was there for the Season. She knew little about Mr Stanton, but he seemed to have little care for town, so she doubted it would matter to him who she invited.

She sat at the small oak escritoire and began to make a list of the families she thought would be beneficial to Olivia and Charlotte for their début. She knew people would wish to attend since the Eastons seldom went to town or entertained. She must admit she was more excited about returning knowing Olivia would be with her, and perhaps she could befriend Charlotte—with no ulterior motives, of course. There were no fewer than one hundred names plus their guests when she was finished, which, she reasoned, was small by *ton* standards.

There was still no word about Gwen or the baby, so she meandered on to the music room to indulge in some time with the pianoforte. She felt a little more excited about the prospect of returning to town, and her music choice reflected her mood. Mozart was more uplifting and jovial than the soulful Beethoven and Bach she had been choosing since her family had departed. By the time she had finished the *Rondo alla Turca*, she glanced at the clock and was surprised to find she had been playing for an hour. She stood and stretched before walking to the window to look out.

Her heart beat a little faster as she observed Mr Stanton talking with Easton on the drive. A groom had brought round a different horse for him since he was leaving Dido. He was stunning as he mounted the horse with ease, a bay gelding that fitted him perfectly. She recalled his unusual amber eyes, which had studied her with vague interest in the parlour, and his loosely-waved dark blond hair framed a face with a strong cleft jaw. He was not as tall as Easton, but he was lean and powerful as she watched him tip his hat and urge the horse forward.

She wanted to know more about him, his quiet reticence and his mysterious demeanour. Why had she never before heard of him? She longed to ask Elly more about him, but knew she would get little more from her. She did think Elly would put them together at every opportunity. She wished she were better equipped with knowledge of this man, in order to deal with her feelings. What if she liked him very well and he had no prospects? Would she like him just as well if he were poor? She was pleasantly surprised to know his lack of title did not diminish his appeal.

Chapter Five

The next day brought a whirlwind of activity, with the birth of Henrietta Elizabeth. Her older sister, Millicent, was not pleased with the new arrival, and the entire household had been doing their best to distract her from wanting her mama. Her nurse had been busy with the baby, and Jolie offered to help since she had no other responsibilities. Jolie loved children, but she had never worked as hard before to make a child happy—not that she had much experience. Thankfully, Andrew came to relieve her of little Millie before she had exhausted every game, trick and song she knew. She had finally relaxed and put her feet up when Olivia burst through the door.

"Oh! Jolie. Where is everyone?" the sprightly young lady asked.

"It is good to see you, Livvy." Jolie stood to embrace her cousin. "Gwen gave birth early this morning. Elly and Nurse have been with Gwen most of the day, and Andrew has only just now relieved me of Millie. Forgive me, but I am fagged," she explained as she ungracefully resumed her place on the sofa.

"Is the baby healthy?" Olivia enquired.

"She appears to be, but I only saw her for a moment," Jolie remarked.

"Another girl?"

"Indeed. Henrietta Elizabeth they are calling her."

Olivia laughed. "Oh, the Dowager will not like that at all. She loathes her name."

"I think it is a beautiful honour to be named after someone. My mother named us for her favourite places in France," Jolie commented.

"At least your names are unique. There were two other Olivias and a half-dozen Elizabeths at school."

"Yes, I suppose so. How was school? Are you happy to be here?" Jolie asked.

"I will miss my friends, of course, but it is always good to be home. Adam said Father is weak and he wishes me to go to London now," she said with a frown.

"Do you not wish to go?"

"I do not wish to leave Father. I would regret missing this time with him. I would have returned from school had I known he was declining again," Olivia said sadly.

"I understand. I think they were concerned about delaying your come-out if the worst happens," Jolie said gently.

"How can I think of it when these may be my last days with Father?" Her honey-coloured curls bounced when she shook her head.

"Perhaps none of us should go," Jolie pondered aloud.

"That will not be necessary," Easton said as he entered the room and embraced his sister, who looked very much like him.

"Why not?" Olivia enquired.

"Father insists on your going now."

"Oh, dear, Adam. Do you think it best?" She looked at him warily.

"It matters not what I think. He has his mind set on it. We believe he still has some time left, but one never knows. We had thought to bring you out with Charlotte at a small party. Perhaps you may form some relationships that will prosper despite the circumstances."

"Very well. If you think it best, I will do as you say."

He smiled lovingly at his little sister, then turned to Jolie. "I had a letter today from my uncle."

"Are my parents well?"

"They write that they arrived safely in Scotland, but do not know how long they intend to remain. It seems Margaux is still determined on her course of action."

"Of course she is," Jolie agreed, knowing her sister to be stubborn to a fault.

"I have had a request for several of our veterans to go to work at an estate, so I may be delayed in joining you in London, but I assure you I will be at the party."

"That is excellent news," Jolie remarked.

"I will save a dance for you, Adam," Olivia said. "But now, I think I shall go and greet Father."

~*~

Two days later, Benedict received word that Mrs Abbott had given birth to another healthy girl, and that the entire Easton household would be removing to London within a se'ennight. Lady Easton had been as good as her word and had included a missive for his mother.

"Mother," Benedict said as he looked up from reading his correspondence at the breakfast table, "Lady Easton has included a letter addressed to you and Charlotte."

"How kind of her," the Duchess said as she took the letter from her son and slid her finger under the seal.

He had said not a word of the plan, in case anything had changed.

His mother was talking out loud as she read. "She is bringing Lady Olivia out sooner than planned, and she has invited Charlotte to be brought out with her."

"That is very obliging of her," Benedict reasoned. The look on his sister's face was not as agreeable.

"I do not consider a small gathering suitable for the daughter of an earl or a duke," his mother said while making a face, which was not quite offended, but not pleased either.

"I would prefer not to come out at all," Charlotte interjected.

"Do you see what I have to deal with, Benedict? Can you please explain to her that she will soon be on the shelf and an old maid? Your bloom will not last and where will you be?" She directed the last at Charlotte.

Benedict only just refrained from throwing his head into his hands. He would prefer to ignore the entire situation.

"Charlotte, why are you opposed to being brought out? If you agree to coming out with Olivia, it will be a much lesser event than your mother would plan, I assure you. Blessedly," he added under his breath.

"I heard that," his mother responded with a severe look.

"I am not comfortable being the centre of attention. I am not beautiful, I am not witty, I am not even fashionable. Do you realise what my figure looks like in the current mode?"

Benedict looked blankly. He knew there was not a proper answer.

"Like a tent!" she exclaimed.

"I am not conceding you look like a tent, mind you, but if you are not comfortable in one style of dress, have the *modiste* make you another," he suggested.

"But then I will attract more notice!" Charlotte said with frustration.

"Lady Easton assures me this will be a small gathering. It is acceptable as a duke's daughter to make your own fashion. If you feel well in what you are wearing, you will find yourself more agreeable. I will not ask you to go to town again if you find this trip displeases you greatly. But I cannot promise I will go to town again myself, should you wish for my escort in the future," he surprised himself by saying. He did not tend to the role of counsellor.

"You are going to town?" his mother asked in astonishment.

"I am."

He could see his sister's mind arguing with itself. But with no better alternative she chose to share the spotlight, rather than be the sole focus of it.

Benedict would not force her to marry. He would provide for her and allow her an independence if she wished it. Their mother insisted she have a Season before he informed Charlotte of this fact. Charlotte was unfashionably eccentric and a bit plumper than was the current mode, but Benedict thought she would take if she made up her mind to dispense with societal approval. She was fortunate to have the luxury.

"I suppose I will go if you will be there. But do not be disappointed if I do not take," she said with a touch of defiance.

"Good girl. I will not force you into anything, Charlotte."

The Duchess stood abruptly and with uncharacteristic motivation. "We must make haste!" She started for the door.

"Why the hurry?" he asked coolly.

"We must leave at once for London and bribe a *modiste*!" she said impatiently before exiting and shouting for her maid.

"It has begun," he said sympathetically towards his sister. Did she have any notion how the family's reputation had suffered a decade ago? He hoped she would not have to find out.

~*~

Benedict departed for London ahead of his sister and mother, who was in a frenzy over packing and finding a suitable wardrobe for her daughter with hardly any notice. He was determined to absent himself from the chaos and ease into this business. And, perhaps, scout the territory before announcing his intentions—if it had not already been spread amongst the town by Ashbury's chit. He had wrongly assumed any of the names on Hughes' list would be open to his proposal. He would remember to question Hughes further on the matter before he further embarrassed himself.

He wanted to be on his way back to his estate within a fortnight. He would ask Hughes to make certain all of the names on the list were sent invitations to the party, subject to Lady Easton's approval, of course. He wanted to be as efficient as possible about the matter and minimise his exposure to the *ton*. Why they were uncommonly fascinated with his family he could not discern. He put his breeches on the same way as any man. Would it matter to someone like Miss Winslow?

Benedict recalled hearing the music before he had departed that day at Wyndham. He had dared to look into the drawing room and had found her lost in Mozart. He had wanted to lose himself too when he listened. She did not merely play the piano—she made it come to life. He was drawn to this woman, and he knew he must distance himself at all costs. It would be a difficult task since she was being brought to town. She would be everywhere the Eastons would be. He could scarcely avoid his oldest friend, nor did he wish to. He had been embarrassed to ask Easton more about her.

He must hurry up with this business arrangement. If he was near her he was certain to make another *mésalliance* and sit in her pocket. He could see the gossip columns now: 'The reclusive Duke did not learn his lesson the first time'. Or there would be a newspaper sketch of her pulling on a leash tied around his neck, while he had his tongue out and salivated like a besotted dog for all passers-by to stop and laugh at.

It was the gossip and his father that had driven him away the first time.

Benedict could never erase the memory of that caricature from his mind, nor the shame. It had not been the ideal way to find out about a philandering wife. His father had never recovered from the disgrace. He had forbidden the marriage and, soon after, the duel and divorce. The duel had taken place in France, where Benedict had sought out Lillian and found her with her lover. He had not mortally wounded the man, but he had died of infection later. Benedict had refused to remain married, and eventually had won a decree of divorce from Parliament. Lillian had reportedly died from disease less than a year later, *may she rot*, he thought bitterly.

His mother had reassured him the scandal had long since passed, but he was not as confident now that the Ashbury girl had refused him.

Chapter Six

Benedict decided he might as well jump in feet first, so he headed to his club the morning after his arrival in town. He rarely made appearances at the club even when he was in town, and his reputation had grown to such epic proportions that some people avoided him or stared at him with awe. The majority of the younger set would have no notion of who he was, let alone what he looked like. That had suited him just fine until now, when it would be useful to slap an old friend on the shoulder and ask for the latest *on-dits* about the available ladies on the market. Then again, he reflected, he preferred his circle to be small and intimate. He had never cared for a wider pool of shallow acquaintances. No matter, he would have to settle for information by proxy or proximity.

He selected a newspaper to hide behind, then chose a chair in the morning room. He was rather close to where he knew the younger bucks preferred to congregate, near to the betting books and the bow window, and he could eavesdrop. However, he was on the early side today for the younger crowd; thus far the only members present were elders discussing politics.

Benedict was about to give up when the older group rose to leave for the afternoon session in the House of Lords. He was folding his paper when he spied a group of three young dandies entering the room. He sat down again promptly, facing away from them, opening his paper and his ears with keen interest. He remembered the routine from his youth: discuss the previous evening's exploits of drinking, women and gaming. It was sometime before the discussion came around to his interest. There was a significant diversion when Lord Alvanley placed a bet for three thousand pounds that one rain drop would reach the bottom of the window before another. Benedict tried to recall why he belonged to a club that had such high standards.

"Have you heard the latest about the Ashbury chits?" asked a young man with a ridiculous waistcoat of lemon-yellow patterned with large red apples.

"Are they returning to town?" Alvanley asked from his seat in the bow window.

"Word is they took Fire to Scotland on a repairing lease," the third interjected.

"Dash it!" The Ridiculous Waistcoated buck mourned.

"You owe me a monkey, Worth," the third goaded.

"What of the other two?" Worth asked curiously.

"I heard Wind went off with her brother to America," the third chimed in again.

"How do you know all of this?" Worth asked sceptically.

"My sister was at school with their cousin," he said, as if that explained everything.

"Did she say anything about Ice?" Worth prodded hopefully.

"She is still on the market, as far as I know. But you know your title is not within her realm."

"Double or nothing I can make her forget she wants to be a duchess," Worth taunted.

"You will have to go much higher to tempt me. You must not have seen the odds lately." The other buck indicated the betting books with a nod of his head.

Benedict was having a difficult time keeping up with the conversation.

Were there actually three daughters? He surmised the daughters had been nicknamed Fire, Wind and Ice, but he had no idea which one he had offered for. Perhaps if he could ascertain which sister wanted to be a duchess, the odds would be in his favour. What was he thinking? He could not simply propose to one sister after being turned down by another. Moreover, it sounded as though two of them were indisposed. He was tempted, however, to prove wrong whichever lady had refused him.

"The only two available dukes are Yardley and Summers," Alvanley said, whilst inspecting his fingernails.

Benedict held the paper higher.

"The former never shows his face. Summers will stick his spoon in the wall any day," Worth said defensively.

"That is often a point in his favour," Alvanley pointed out.

"No, I do not believe it of Ice. She will accept me, one of these days," Worth said confidently.

"She must have some warm blood in her, being half French. I cannot believe the layer of ice is unbreakable."

"She's warm enough, as long as you do not propose to her."

Benedict nearly spewed his coffee. *French*?

He cared not who saw him. He stood up, threw down his paper and stormed towards the door. Barely stopping for his hat and coat, he could feel the gazes of the three dandies burning into his back as he withdrew.

He walked hastily towards his house, muttering and cursing the entire way. Hughes had lost his mind—and likely his post. The Ashbury girl must be a rare beauty indeed for Hughes to have risked his wrath. There had better be a very good reason for that gentleman putting him in a humiliating position again. The butler held open the door as Benedict was still seething.

"Send Hughes in to me, now," he said in a deadly calm tone, although his blood was boiling.

When Hughes entered the room a few moments later, Benedict tried to remind himself what a loyal, dependent, hard worker Hughes was.

"Your Grace?"

"Would you care to explain to me why you felt it acceptable to include Ashbury's daughter on the list?" he asked in the quiet, meticulous voice which was a warning to anyone who knew him well.

"If I may be so bold, your Grace, I included all three daughters, to be precise. Lord Ashbury is possessed of three girls; triplets in point of fact. All are well-bred and highly accomplished, in addition to being uncommon beauties. But their *mother* is French," said the secretary, the last word barely audible, yet, clearly indicative of his thoughts on Benedict's prejudice. "However, their father is English, and they have been residing in England since the horrors with Napoleon."

French. Benedict heard not another word after that. Lillian had been French. He pondered in silence until he could speak. "Would you be so kind as to tell me which Ashbury daughter I've already offered for? Fire, Wind, or Ice?" he said in a mocking tone.

"Beaujolais, your Grace. I believe she is the one referred to as Ice."

Somehow, that made everything worse. The one who wanted to be a duchess. He could have prevented much had he bothered to read the names on the list. What a fool he would look when the gossips heard she had refused him.

"What are the other two named?" he asked, almost knowing them to be equally blatant before he heard them.

"Lady Margaux and Lady Anjou," Hughes pronounced their Christian names with a flawless French accent. "However, it would seem they are now spoken for: a recent occurrence, I believe, since the original list was written. I did not think they would be of interest to you any longer in light of their sister's—ah—sentiments."

Benedict cursed his own stupidity.

"And you did not think it prudent to mention this to me, or to ascertain that the offer would be welcome to Lady Beaujolais beforehand?"

"I beg your pardon. I assumed you had read the list. And the offer was made to Lady Beaujolais because…" Hughes trailed off, clearly thinking better of mentioning it was common knowledge she was holding out for the highest title.

"She wants to be a duchess. Yes, I have heard," Benedict finished for him.

Hughes stood awaiting his Grace.

"You may go, Hughes. I have no further need of you."

Benedict sat staring at the swirled, chartreuse-coloured designs in the wallpaper for some time, seriously debating letting his title revert to the Crown upon his death. After all, it would not matter to him in the afterlife. But there would be many people affected adversely, his conscience argued. Many thoughts crossed his mind as he began to sketch his own caricature for the newspapers, this time with himself having a pea for a brain.

Was everyone associated with France to be damned because of Lillian? He was inclined to think French women looked upon love and marriage differently, though he had to acknowledge his experience was limited. It did not mean he was willing to experiment again in order to satisfy the question.

He did, however, want a glimpse of this *nonpareil* who wanted to be a duchess—yet not his duchess.

~*~

"The jonquil or the pomona green?" Olivia held up the fabrics for Jolie's opinion.

"Maybe the jonquil, but the green makes you look sallow."

"Sallow sounds like sour food. No, thank-you," Olivia said as she put the green back on the table.

"This shade of periwinkle is very becoming," Elly said as she held it up to Olivia's cheek.

"If you think it is light enough to be acceptable, I like it very well," Olivia agreed.

"I do. Perhaps one more gown for the theatre and a new riding habit, and you should have enough to manage the remainder of the Season," Elly said, glancing at the clock.

"Do you need to leave?" Jolie asked. "I can help Olivia finish here if you wish."

"I was hoping to be home in time to ride with the children. They are not listening to the grooms as they should and I want to supervise."

"Of course, we do not mind in the least," Olivia reassured her.

"Thank you, I will send the carriage back directly," Elly said as she took her leave.

After the fabrics had been chosen, the ladies began to look over the latest fashion plates to choose suitable patterns.

"You have excellent taste," the *modiste*, Madame Monique, remarked to Jolie as she assisted Olivia.

"I do wonder when the waistlines will drop again. They can scarcely go any higher," Jolie remarked as she held up a dress to Olivia.

"What goes up must come down, of course," Madame Monique said

56

with a sly smile.

"If we could only go to Paris," Jolie said wistfully.

"That is not necessary," a heavily-accented voice said from behind them.

"Ah, Madame Clement," the *modiste* greeted another French customer.

The ladies turned to discover an incredibly beautiful, fascinating female standing before them. She was dressed in a gown with the waist at its natural level.

"As you can see, I am making her a dress of the latest Parisian fashion and the waist is not so high," Madame Monique pointed out.

"Are you recently from Paris?" Jolie asked.

"Within the last week. You may help bring the fashion here, *non*?" Madame Clement suggested.

Jolie was delighted, and the two broke out in furious French. They began discussing Paris, and before long they had moved to mutual acquaintances.

Olivia turned to the *modiste* and immediately decided to change all of her patterns to the new style.

Madame indicated for her assistant, Jemima, to measure both of the ladies.

"I will likely be in mourning soon, so I may as well enjoy the fashion whilst I can," she reasoned.

"The new style suits you very well. Your figure can carry either style well. Many are not so fortunate," the seamstress remarked.

"I am thankful. But in fact, I have a friend who will be pleased with this latest style. Perhaps I should recommend you to her," Olivia added thoughtfully.

Such comments being music to the ears of any *modiste*, Madame smiled. "Any friend of Lady Olivia's is always very welcome."

The ladies took their leave, and climbed into the carriage.

"Did you discover you knew Madame Clement?" Olivia asked with curiosity.

"No, but we have many mutual friends in France. Is she not delightful? And it will be a coup for you to début in the latest mode!"

"A fortunate coincidence, indeed. Charlotte ought to be told as well. It would not be fair for me to steal the thunder at our mutual come-out."

"You are very good, Olivia. Should we call on her on our way home?"

"Oh, no," Olivia said hastily. "She does not care for surprises," she added lamely. "I will send a note to see when is convenient."

"I cannot wait to have a dress with a waist again," Jolie said, returning to the main subject.

"It was very gracious for Madame to accommodate us so quickly."

"It seems so, but it will do her more good than us, I assure you," Jolie added, knowing they were likely benefiting the *modiste* by setting a trend.

The carriage turned through the gates of Hyde Park, and Jolie returned some waves to acquaintances on their way back to Wyndham House.

"Is that Mr Stanton?" Jolie asked, squinting at a figure on a horse some distance ahead.

"Perhaps. It is too far away to know for certain," Olivia remarked, sounding evasive.

"Should we move closer? I should not wish to unintentionally snub him," Jolie suggested.

"Is it proper for me to be seen much before next week? Perhaps we should return directly."

"Of course. I had merely thought you to be long-time acquaintances."

Olivia brushed the comment away with her hand. "Oh, we are, but you never know who we might run into if we stop."

"Very well," Jolie said, masking her disappointment. "Are there any other diversions you would enjoy while in London? I adore the theatre."

"I would enjoy the theatre and perhaps a few balls would be nice," Olivia said thoughtfully.

"I've no doubt you will be inundated with invitations the moment you are out," Jolie reassured her.

"Is it very difficult, being out? I remember hearing Elly talk about the gossip and the competition," Olivia asked worriedly.

"There is truth in what you heard. You must develop a thick skin. This is my fifth Season, and there are all sorts of things being bandied around about 'the triplets'. We have been nicknamed Fire, Wind and Ice, and there are many kinds of bets on the books about who we will or will not marry, in addition to the gossip amongst the female set."

"How do you know of these things?" Olivia asked in dismay.

"Some you overhear, and much was told us by Charles."

"I do not think Adam would know those things," Olivia said, concentrating. "Which one are you?"

"Ice. Many thought me pretentious in the beginning, but now I think it has something to do with not accepting marriage proposals," Jolie said with a laugh.

Olivia stared at her, wide-eyed.

"Please do not condemn me, Livvy. If you had seen those making the proposals, you would not judge me too harshly."

"Is it difficult having been out for so many Seasons? I heard them saying you turned down Yardley," Olivia said shyly.

"Yes, I am on the shelf," Jolie answered while looking off in the distance. "But with Yardley, it was more about the manner of his proposal."

"I would not have told him no," Olivia replied boldly, yet her cheeks were flushed.

Chapter Seven

Olivia had to practically sneak from the house to visit Charlotte alone. There was little chance she would be able to keep Benedict's identity from Jolie if she went to their home. She was not certain she agreed with Elly about her plan, but she did not know how else to make it any better. She wished she was as confident it would all turn out for the best.

She was shown into the parlour, where the Duchess was partaking of tea and toast in a languorous fashion upon a crocodile chaise in a light pink dressing gown adorned with feathers. Olivia had always liked the Duchess, but could certainly understand why she was considered peculiar. She could not imagine any female of her acquaintance who would dare to be seen, let alone entertain guests, in such a fashion.

"Lady Olivia! So good of you to call," the Duchess said, in a manner belying her slothful pose.

"Good morning, your Grace, I trust you are well?" Olivia asked, fearing she was in for a monologue of indispositions, yet was aware she could not avoid it.

"Oh, as well as can be. Benedict is here, as you have likely heard, and has managed to convince Charlotte to be brought out, so I shall not think of myself until the Season is over. I suppose you know all of this, since you are being brought out together. Did you come to see Charlotte?"

"I did. Is she home?" Olivia enquired.

"Is she home? She has not set foot from the house since we arrived in town. She sent her maid to the lending library, and continues as she did in the country."

"She always did have a taste for the literary," Olivia said fondly.

"If one can call novels literary," the Duchess said doubtfully, though not in a condemnatory fashion.

"Do you think she will see me?"

"Of course, my dear." The Duchess reached over to pull the bell-rope, and instructed the butler to have Lady Charlotte sent for.

"Please let Lady Easton know I am at her disposal, should she wish for any assistance. I do not wish to be underfoot and meddling, however."

"My cousin is helping her, and I believe they have matters in hand. But I will certainly pass on your offer."

"Which cousin?" the Duchess asked with interest.

"Beaujolais," Olivia replied tentatively, wondering how much the Duchess knew about the failed proposal. Thankfully they were interrupted before she was quizzed further on the matter.

When Charlotte entered the room, Olivia had to hide her surprise. She had not seen Charlotte in almost a year, when she had left the finishing school. Charlotte had changed, to put it mildly. She had always been more round than most of their peers, but she looked as if she had added two stone to her frame, and she had let her hair go wild. Charlotte's nose was in a book as she walked in. Olivia wanted to shake her and ask where her old friend was hiding.

"Charlotte?" Olivia asked, interrupting Charlotte since her mother did not seem to want to bother herself with the task.

"Livvy?" Charlotte looked up from the pages with surprise. She placed a bookmark and set the book down on the nearby table.

Olivia held out her arms to greet her. "How are you?"

Charlotte blushed. "I am well."

The two sat on a sofa as the Duchess continued to ply herself with toast.

"I wanted to see if you had ordered your wardrobe," Olivia began. "I was at the *modiste's* yesterday, and heard tell the fashions are changing."

"Are they indeed?" the Duchess bestirred herself to ask.

"I hope this is good news," Charlotte muttered.

"We met a Madame Clement, recently arrived from Paris, and she was wearing the most dashing gown with a low waist." Olivia indicated the style with her hands.

"But will it be an improvement on the current fashion?" the Duchess asked sceptically as she glanced at her daughter's curves, similar to her own.

"I think it will be an improvement. Madame Clement looked stunning. Perhaps you should see my *modiste* and ask her opinion?" Olivia suggested.

"I would be delighted if you could convince Charlotte to do anything!" the Duchess said doubtfully.

Olivia could not help but think the apples were falling near the tree. "I would be happy to go with you, Charlotte," she offered handsomely. "I am also considering a new coiffure. Perhaps we can début in the new mode together and set a fashion."

"I will go with you to the *modiste*," Charlotte said hesitantly. "But I doubt I will look like anything more than a sack of potatoes near you, dear Livvy."

"Oh, pish! We are made differently, 'tis true, but one can make the most of what one has. Men prefer different types, or the world would be a bore. One man's pleasure is another's pain, they say."

"Do you really believe that rubbish?" Charlotte asked.

"I do. Let me help you for the come-out and see if I am not right," Olivia said daringly.

The Duchess looked at her daughter, wondering how she would respond. Charlotte looked out the window longingly for a minute, then at her hands before looking at Olivia again.

"Very well, I will do it."

~*~

Jolie decided to walk to the park when she discovered Olivia had gone out earlier in the morning. She welcomed the time to think and feed the birds. The trees were in full leaf and the pathways were lined with fragrant blooms of lilies and peonies. Her maid stayed discreetly in the distance, and she chose a bench near the Serpentine. There was something calming about water that helped her relax. Not that she had anything taxing her, other than the stark reminder that she had been out for five Seasons. Five. Hearing Olivia say it out loud had made it reverberate in her head ever since. Was it too late for her, now? Had she ruined all of her chances? She was not like Margaux—she did not prefer the thought of living alone. Yet, she had not found anyone she could live with. What did that say about her?

Perhaps she needed to reconsider her priorities. Nothing had been as she had imagined it would be when she had first made her début. Although she and her sisters had had more suitors than they could count, none had been the dashing, confident beau she had dreamt about. She did not think her desires so unrealistic. She truly would have accepted an arrangement had her father planned one. She trusted his judgement, though she did not trust her own. What would her father consider important if he were to choose?

First, she decided, she needed security. That eliminated every gambler with his pockets to let, which was more than half of the prospective suitors. She tossed some bread crumbs to the geese approaching her.

Second, she would choose someone she could respect. This caused her to wrinkle her nose and purse her lips in thought. She respected her father, and Easton and Wyndham, and the soldiers who had fought in the war. But she was finding it difficult to think of any others who might earn her admiration. Most of her suitors found it humorous to participate in curricle races or watch cock-fights. Maybe she should look for a politician. She could be a good political hostess, she thought, tossing more crumbs. Third, she would prefer to hold her spouse in some affection, but as long as she was not repulsed by him, she should open her mind. She must, or she would find herself with her sister in Scotland. Though at least they would have each other there, she reassured herself.

"Mademoiselle Winslow! It is a surprise to find you here," Madame Clement said as she approached from the pathway.

"I come here often," Jolie said with a smile to her new friend. "I enjoy feeding the birds."

"Do I disturb you? You look lost in thought," the Frenchwoman remarked.

"Oh, not at all," Jolie reassured. "I was thinking, but I am happy to see you."

"Do you go to the theatre?" Madame asked, and Jolie thought perhaps she might not have many friends in London.

"I adore the theatre, but my cousin is not yet out, so we must wait."

"I hope, then, that it is not too long to wait!"

"Only a few more days," Jolie reassured the woman. "I am helping her prepare for her come-out. Oh! Would you care to come? I will be happy to send an invitation."

"That is very considerate of you. I confess, I have very few acquaintances in London," Madame said frankly.

"It is my pleasure. I am certain my cousins will not mind."

Madame Clement handed Jolie her card with her direction, and the ladies parted. Jolie began to stroll back towards the house with her maid in tow, trying to consider some of her suitors in a new light, but still finding them wanting.

"Miss Jolie?"

She looked up to find Mr Stanton almost directly in front of her. She rarely saw anyone on this path, yet today she had seen two acquaintances within a few minutes.

"Good day, Mr Stanton." She dropped a curtsy to his bow.

"I trust I find you well?" he said with politeness.

"I am, thank you. I was not minding my way, however. I am unaccustomed to meeting many other souls along this path, though you are the second today," she confessed.

"Yes, it is what I appreciate most about it," he said brusquely.

"I suppose so. I prefer to think of it as a garden of heaven amongst the chaos. Although, I own, I miss it when I am away from it."

"Do you?" he said, looking bored.

That was a reaction she was unused to from the male sex.

"Is your sister looking forward to the party?" she asked, searching for something to interest him.

"I would not phrase it just so, but she is, I believe, at this very moment soliciting the talents of a *modiste*."

"I do believe my cousin Olivia called on Charlotte this morning about that very thing."

He gave a half-smile laced with indifference, and Jolie felt disappointed she was unable to engage him. She felt it keenly in light of her recent reflections. Perhaps she was past her bloom. She was beginning to feel her previous rejection of Yardley to be premature, though that door was now firmly closed, thanks to her scathing refusal.

"May I beg the honour of a dance with you?" she heard him ask as she was pondering her dim future.

"I—I would be honoured, thank you," she replied, startled by the request.

"Until then. Good day, Miss Jolie."

"Good day, Mr Stanton."

He tipped his hat and walked off briskly, leaving her staring after him in bewilderment.

Chapter Eight

Benedict was in a foul mood. He had just come from a meeting with Hughes and his solicitor, and had discovered the marriage list had dwindled substantially. Three of the names on it had been those of the Ashbury sisters, and three others had since become betrothed to others as the Season drew near its end. That left scarce few Eligibles, and he'd had the ill fortune to hear Lady Mary titter. He had debated walking straight to Carlton House and begging to relinquish the dukedom that very moment.

As if that were not enough, he thought he had seen someone from the past walking down a secluded path in the park and he had followed, almost running into Miss Jolie. He had been so distracted and angry he had been unconscionably rude to her. Yet again, she had not looked like a poor relation, and in hindsight, he realised he must speak with Easton about her. However, she could have little of merit to say about his behaviour and would likely make excuses when it came time for his dance. He doubted not she would have the young Corinthian and dandy sets at her feet. But, with little prospects, none would be serious suitors. If she truly had no prospects, that was.

He must speak to Easton, or erase her from his mind. He had been squandering entirely too much time daydreaming of her when he should have been attending to the business at hand. He would send a note around to Easton to see if he would join him at Gentleman Jackson's for a round of fisticuffs, as in the old days. He could attempt to enquire about the cousin then before meeting her again.

He walked onward back to Stanton Place to meet someone his mother deemed suitable, over tea. The other remaining ladies on the list had accepted the invitations to the party at the Eastons'. He stopped abruptly on the path. *She still calls me Mr Stanton*, he realised, wondering if it would change her attitude towards him once she discovered him to be a duke. He hoped not. There was something refreshing about her, and if she either snubbed or toadied up to him, it would end the fantasy his imagination had perpetuated.

Benedict strode into the parlour where his mother was holding court, and the scene was worse than he could have imagined. His mother's oldest friend, Lady Edgeworth, and her daughter, who looked to be no more than four and ten years of age, were awaiting him; he had to be almost two decades her senior and was not amused in the least. He greeted the ladies and settled in for an afternoon of biscuits and boredom.

~*~

Jolie barely made it to the drawing room in time for the guests to proceed to dinner. She was not the guest of honour, nor required for the receiving line, so she had focused on Olivia's appearance thinking she would not be missed. She dearly wanted a glimpse of Mr Stanton in evening attire, and to meet his sister. However, the evening was young and this was hardly to be a crush by *ton* standards.

She had a gown in the new style for herself, made of sarsenet with a silk overlay, but had chosen a bolder blue then what would be considered appropriate for a début. Five Seasons should have earned her some colour, she thought reproachfully.

She took the arm of the last male in the line for dinner, who happened to be one of her more flamboyant swains, Sir Percival Jones.

"Lady Beaujolais! A sight for sore eyes, to be sure. I was afraid you had not come back after all," he said, kissing her hand in dramatic fashion despite his ear-high collar points.

"Hello, Sir Percy. I trust you have come to no harm in my absence?" she leaned in to ask.

"No more than usual," he assured her. "I say, I see you and Lady Olivia mean to set a new trend," he remarked as he studied her through his quizzing glass; it accentuated the gold flecks in his magnified eye.

"Well, does it meet with the approval of the Beau Monde expert?" she asked as she tolerated his scrutiny. "It is the latest kick from Paris; I have it on first-hand authority," she assured him.

"I would never question your taste, my dear. I only ponder the resulting effects on those without your figure to recommend them," he countered.

"I will take that as a compliment," she said, smiling.

"Speaking of figures, is it true you took lessons from the Gentleman? It was Byron's choice for keeping trim."

She laughed. "I cannot divulge all of my secrets."

"I cannot have a small morsel?" he begged.

"Very well. I might have sparred with him a time or two in the company of my sisters."

"I'll say. I'll say!" he beamed with admiration.

She shook her head. "Come now, we are not the only ladies to practice sparring."

"Maybe not, but I find it fantastic. Shall we?" he asked as he held out his arm to escort her.

There were fifty for dinner, and Jolie was seated at the opposite end of the grand table from Mr Stanton. He was surrounded by marriageable misses, she thought uncharitably, but remembered Elly had mentioned he was in town to find a wife and had likely requested introductions. She tried to smile at her court, seated around her, while trying to steal glimpses of Mr Stanton's mother and sister, though the golden *epergnes* filled with flowers made the task nigh impossible.

"What do you think of Yardley's sister?" Sir Percival asked, without disguising his curiosity.

"Yardley's sister is here?" Jolie asked somewhat surprised. She had not recalled seeing her on the guest list.

"She is the one on Easton's left. She has quite a pretty face but has curves more suited to the Cyprian set," he whispered in her ear.

"Sir Percy!" Jolie remonstrated with a teasing rap on his knuckles. "You are not to say those things to a lady."

"Aye, and a lady should not know what it means. But 'tis still the truth," he said without remorse.

Jolie was inclined to agree as she cast a glance at the young lady down the table. She would not mind some of those curves herself, she thought somewhat enviously. "It will not hurt the daughter of a duke as long as she does not act like a Cyprian," she remarked.

"True enough. Perhaps I should make her acquaintance and ask for a set. I am certain Yardley will not be stingy with settlements."

"No indeed," Jolie muttered, thinking about the settlement he had offered her.

"I never thought to see him in society again, but I suppose it is on account of squiring his sister about," Sir Percy said, philosophically for him.

Jolie choked on her wine.

"Are you all right, my dear?"

She nodded while her eyes watered, trying not to draw attention to herself. Yardley must be here, she thought in alarm. He is here, and no one had bothered to inform her. It had been one thing to refuse him when she had thought she would never see him again. She began to feel sick and wanted to flee the room. That was the last thing she could or would do, of course. She suffered through dinner, dying to crane her neck and peer down the table to locate the odious, insufferable duke.

When she happened to turn to her dinner partner on the left, she did not think she had seen anyone who might be Yardley. But she could not very well ignore Lord Macon, so she would have to wait through this interminable meal.

When it was time to move to the ballroom for dancing, Jolie was anxious to position herself to hear the introductions and watch the receiving line as the remainder of guests entered. There were more people than she had anticipated; obviously the guest list had been adjusted considerably after her initial making of it, for she'd had no idea Yardley and his family would be present. However, she should not have expected them to be excluded since they were friends of the Eastons.

She walked around the perimeter, greeting acquaintances as she scanned feverishly for the unfamiliar face she was desperate to see, yet avoid. She saw another of her admirers making his way across the room towards her, but as she quickly turned to go in the other direction, she heard the ominous sound of fabric ripping. An audible sigh escaped her. Experience told her it was a tear she would have to mend at once. But she had wanted to see Olivia's face when she saw the surprise that awaited her. She hastily left the ballroom to find her maid to mend the damage. She would miss the announcements and thus the discreet discovery of Yardley's identity. She needed to return in time for the second set and her promised dance with Mr Stanton. She smiled in anticipation. She determined to enjoy the set and put all thoughts of Yardley and his distasteful offer out of her mind.

By the time she returned to the ballroom, the quadrille was nearing its close. She found Elly and made her way to her side, thinking Mr Stanton would look for her there.

"Where have you been?" Elly enquired.

"I tore my flounce. Thank heavens Jenkins is genius with a needle."

"Gracious! Who was the exuberant partner?"

"Myself. I was fleeing Snodgrass in haste," Jolie confessed.

"Then I would call that a fortunate happenstance," Elly retorted.

"Have you seen Mr Stanton? I am engaged for the next set with him," Jolie explained.

"He is dancing with his sister." Elly indicated with her head.

"Of course. Was Livvy much surprised to see my uncle?" Jolie asked, trying to glimpse Mr Stanton and his sister on the floor.

"She was, though I did not expect the waterworks. Perhaps we would have been best to bring him in at dinner, though it does appear that Adam has managed to laugh her out of it," Elly remarked.

"I will find Uncle after this set. Is he looking well?"

"Surprisingly so. He was thrilled to see Livvy out, though I am certain he will suffer for it later."

The set was ending, and Jolie's heart began to race at the anticipation of the dance with Mr Stanton. One would think she was unaccustomed to this. Five Seasons, she reminded herself and smiled as he walked toward her with Yardley's sister. She wrinkled her brow and opened her mouth to enquire where Yardley was in the throng, when she was pre-empted by Elly.

"Ah, here is one of the ladies of the evening. Lady Charlotte Stanton, may I present my cousin, Lady Beaujolais Winslow?"

Jolie knew her mouth was gaping as she put the pieces together. She trembled and felt a betraying flush spread over her body as her cousin nudged her. Somehow, she managed to curtsy and look up to Lady Charlotte.

"It is a pleasure to make your acquaintance, Lady Charlotte." Jolie hoped her voice did not betray her. She could not look at Mr Stanton.

"I do not believe we have had a proper introduction either. Lady Easton, would you do the honours?" she heard him say brusquely. Dear God, let it not be so.

"Your Grace, please allow me to introduce you to Lady Beaujolais Winslow. Lady Beaujolais, his Grace, the Duke of Yardley," Elly said quietly.

Jolie was forced to turn towards him as she felt as if all eyes were on her, but she could not make herself look at him. She curtsied deeply. She felt Elly's hand steady her.

"I believe this is my dance?" he surprised her by saying, and she looked up to find his hand extended to her.

Chapter Nine

"Perhaps you would rather rot in hell then dance with me, but I would prefer not to make a scene here. You may cut up at me later if you wish," he remarked curtly as he led her to the dance floor.

Jolie cringed at her own words being recited back to her as she stared at his cravat. She said nothing and could barely focus on her footsteps; her mind and emotions were being pulled into an abyss she feared she could not climb out of. She was still trembling, and he was ever so close. She could feel his warmth almost suffocating her ability to think. She had never felt so humiliated or embarrassed.

"It would perhaps be good to force a smile, if it is not beyond your abilities. As you can imagine, the crowd is watching to see with whom I am dancing after such a long time away," he said, his tone cold and bitter.

She met his eyes for the first time. They held nothing but loathing. That fact made it easier for her to regain her composure. "I did not know who you were, sir," she replied with a false smile.

"That much is mutual. I do not know why the Eastons felt it necessary to perpetrate this hoax, but it is done."

"I imagine the blame for that is mine. I placed them in a difficult position," Jolie confessed.

"Ah, with my very unwelcome proposal. I beg your pardon," he said scornfully as he inclined his head and looked away.

She could feel her anger building again. "I am flattered, I am sure, but I am unaccustomed to receiving proposals from those with whom I have no acquaintance."

"From what I have heard, you accept no proposals," he countered icily.

"That was most gentlemanly of you," she said sarcastically and tried to pull away.

"No, you do not." He pulled her closer to him with a tight grip. "You will suffer through this along with me. Both of us are behaving childishly and have put on a grand show for the tabbies. But you will not confirm it by deserting me on the floor. I will leave you by Lady Easton's side when the dance ends and we end our acquaintance then," he said with an authority that was accustomed to being obeyed.

"And miss my chance to cut up at you? I think not," she countered with a slight shake of her head. She could feel him stiffen.

"Of course, if you have more words to say, although you have made your point quite sufficiently."

"Do not discount the therapeutic effect of releasing venom. The French have that part right," she added scathingly.

The Duke said not another word. Jolie said not another word. This was the longest waltz she had ever suffered through. But she would have a few words to say to her cousins when this was finished. Waltzes were not to be played at a début when débutantes were not permitted to waltz, yet here she was in the arms of her adversary.

She chose to look about her and noticed her new acquaintance had arrived. Madame Clement was wearing a dashing gown of canary that stood out vibrantly amongst the white and blacks of the crowd.

The Duke also spied her at the same time as the dance ended and they walked off the floor.

"Good God! Lillian? This is not possible! How could she…?" His voice trailed off.

"I invited her," Jolie said defiantly, though she noticed his face had turned deathly pale. "Madame Clement, how lovely to see you." She painted her Society smile into place.

"I see you are acquainted with my charming ex-husband," the woman smiled, speaking in a sultry voice.

Yardley stood as still as a statue and without saying a word. Jolie wanted to hide as the realisation hit her. Spinsterhood in Scotland looked more appealing every moment. How had she unknowingly befriended Yardley's former wife, who was supposed to be dead, and refused the proposal of the very same man—the first man she was ever interested in?

The crowd had separated and was whispering as Elly came up to them. "Why do we not move this reunion to the parlour? I am certain everyone has much to say to each other. In private," she said, with a voice that indicated a command, not a suggestion.

"*Oui,* a good idea," Madame Clement said, taking Jolie's arm.

Elly took hold of Yardley's and began to walk from the ballroom. He still had not said a word. The crowd parted and Jolie did her best to look unaffected. The Duchess of Yardley was in a chair at the side of the ballroom, fanning herself—or being fanned.

Elly chose the parlour near the entrance. Once they were behind closed doors, she did not mince her words.

"Madame, I do believe it best if you take your leave. My cousin is very kind-hearted and quick to include everyone, but she was unaware of your history. As you can see it is a difficult time for you to make your entrée back from the dead. I would not wish to take away from Lady Olivia or Lady Charlotte's night. Lady Beaujolais can see you out. Good evening," Elly said as tactfully as she could in the circumstances.

Jolie did not want to be in the room with either person and thought it best to take her leave, too. Yardley, however, beat her to it.

"Thank you for the dance, Lady Beaujolais. Your servant," he said as he bowed, and left the room without a word to his former wife.

"I beg your pardon, Madame. I could not have imagined." Jolie turned toward the lady, crestfallen.

"*Non*. I do not suppose it would have occurred to you," Madame Clement answered demurely. "I did not know he would be present, of course. It was whispered he did not go out in Society any longer."

"He has only just returned," Jolie answered.

"I was unaware he thought me dead," Madame replied, unperturbed.

"I have only heard rumours. I have not spoken with him about you," Jolie said warily.

"*Oui*, that is the English way. To whisper behind backs and pretend nothing happened to the faces," Madame said scathingly.

Jolie knew there was some truth to what she said, but remained silent.

"I suppose all is ruined for me here, now," Madame said, falling theatrically onto the sofa and looking even more beautiful when distraught. "I had hoped Benedict might be willing to help me, but I see he is not prepared to forgive."

Jolie strongly suspected she was correct in that assumption. "Perhaps he might be willing to speak with you. If he thought you dead, you can imagine his astonishment," she reasoned.

"*Peut être,*" Madame replied, considering Jolie's words.

"What do you need help with? Is there something I might do for you?" Jolie asked, knowing she was likely to regret it, but she felt bad for this woman.

"*Bien sur*, money. It is always money!" Madame said throwing up her hands. "He left me with nothing, as did Monsieur Clement. And it appears Benedict has left my reputation in ruins in London too. I had hoped to open my own establishment here. I am not afraid of work as are the English *ton*," she said condemningly.

Jolie desperately wanted to ask more about Yardley, but she dared not. This was obviously a woman scorned.

"He killed my friend, in a duel over me. Did you know that? He was so obsessed with me, he was jealous of everything. You might want to consider the man he is before you are tempted to become a duchess. It is not worth the price, I promise you," Madame said scathingly.

"He is not interested in marrying me," Jolie said with confidence.

"You are naïve, but I tell you this because you have been kind to me." Madame sighed deeply. "I will go for tonight. I will consider writing him a letter. Perhaps he will read it and have compassion for me. Even if it is only to be rid of me," she said pitifully.

"I am sorry, Madame," Jolie said genuinely. She did not know the whole of the story, but it was easy to believe there was some truth in what the Frenchwoman said.

~*~

Jolie returned to the parlour after seeing Madame Clement out. She was hardly in the mood to return to the ballroom, and was thankful she had not promised any more sets. She opened the side doors that led out to the terrace and listened to the gaiety and the music from the dancing. She was trying to reason through the hurt she felt. She knew her cousins would never play a joke on her to be hateful, but she could not imagine why they had done this to her. There was no good explanation she could come up with, since they knew who Yardley was.

Several things came to mind that perpetuated the deception, including the omission of their titles upon introduction. It had to have been deliberate, though she had thought nothing of it at the time. She had put

79

her cousins in an untenable situation, however, by refusing Yardley's proposal. Perhaps that was why they had done it.

She had to admit to herself she was not only hurt by the deceit about Yardley. Her emotions were in turmoil over finding out that Madame Clement was his former wife. Nothing good would come of furthering her relationship with the Duke—even if he was not repulsed by her. It was very probable the old scandal would resurface, and distancing herself was for the best. But she was melancholic at the thought of Mr Stanton's removal from her life.

She knew she had to face Yardley eventually, and she wanted to be unaffected. She regretted her hasty words, which had been thrown back in her face, but she had done the right thing in refusing Yardley. She doubted everything she knew about him, however, yet it did not make her less confused or hurt. Then, of all things, for her to have invited his former wife tonight! She brought her hands to her face in recollection. He must truly hate her now, if he did not already. She was ashamed to face him.

"May I join you?" Elly asked quietly from behind her as she stood gazing out of the doors.

Jolie nodded without speaking. Her throat was swelling with unshed tears, and she did not want to be upset. *Ladies do not yell. Ladies do not yell*, she kept telling herself, because she wanted to yell at Elly this very moment.

Elly put her arm around Jolie. "Can you forgive me? It does not seem like it now, but we did what we thought was best."

Jolie shook her head and searched for a handkerchief.

Elly handed her one and continued talking. "We thought if you had the chance to know one another, as we know both of you, it would change your minds," she explained.

"I do not know what to say. I do not understand why you felt the need to deceive me. I feel a fool."

"I would feel the same way. I am sorry. Adam and I thought—no think—" Elly corrected, "you both are well suited. We had little time to consider between your refusal of his offer and his arrival."

"It matters not now. If I had not made sure of it before, I certainly did tonight!"

"He will not blame you for inviting her, Jolie. You could not have known. We have all thought her dead these ten years past," Elly said, trying to comfort her.

"It is not even that, though it was a stunning work of coincidence," Jolie said. "He threw my words back in my face. He made it very clear what he thought of me and my refusal of him."

Elly hugged her tight. "Oh, dear. I am sorry. I suppose he was more hurt than I realised. He is usually the consummate gentleman."

"I am flattered to have brought out his inner beast," Jolie said derisively, while dabbing at her eyes with a handkerchief.

"Are you feeling well enough to return to the ballroom?"

"No, thank you. Please make my excuses if necessary." She was not going to yell at her cousin, but she was not ready to relinquish her mortification.

~*~

Why was she not returning to the ballroom? An entire set had passed and there was no sign of her. Benedict looked about for Lady Easton and saw her enter and return to her husband's side, but not Lady Beaujolais. He was furious, and he debated the wisdom of speaking about it until he had cooled down. Marching over to Easton and planting him a facer would only add to his ill repute—though it would certainly make him feel better. He had been made a laughing-stock again, and Easton was partially responsible. He could not credit it. Of course, no one could have foreseen the reappearance of Lillian. He had not yet grasped the reality of it all. She was alive. Was it not a bad dream? Or was it his penance when, at last, he had chosen to put the past behind him? What impeccable timing! It was a scene the Bard himself could have written, or at least appreciated.

He could not tolerate another dance at the moment, notwithstanding the necessity of meeting more candidates for his duchess. He was not good at small talk even when at his best. He chose the solace of the terrace and the fresh air. He heard the sounds of a piano coming from the parlour at the front of the house and felt his feet moving towards it, despite his better judgement.

She was playing with her eyes closed. Her cheeks were stained from tears, and he was intruding on an intimate moment of emotion, but he could not leave. He was intoxicated by the feelings evoked by the haunting, mournful song, which expressed words more eloquent than any he could summon. There were so many things he wished to say, but he could not erase the past. And he did not think she would wish to hear a word of it.

The music stopped with a clash of keys, and his trance stopped. He gazed at her with her head in her hands over the keys. He stepped into the room and made his presence known by a slight cough. He gave her a moment to compose herself before going further into the room. He did not speak. She wanted to say her well-deserved words and he would let her.

"You!"

He inclined his head and narrowed his eyes.

She stood and marched towards him with her fists balled. He had to admire the fire in her eyes. There was nothing cold about this woman.

She said not another word, but took one of those balled fists and punched him in the gut.

He let out a small grunt of surprise and pain.

"How dare you!" she demanded. She made as if to hit him again, and he took hold of her wrists.

"Use your words," he said condescendingly.

"You want words?" She pulled her hands away. "You want words?" She began to pace the room.

He stood silent, watching her looking more beautiful than ever as she towered in rage.

"You are the most dastardly, high-handed, condescending, pompous…arrogant…self-important…" she trailed off at a loss for adjectives and threw her hands in the air.

"Again, I beg your pardon. Have you done?" It would do little good to refute her claims.

She looked up at him with exasperation and turned her back on him.

"I am done." He turned quietly and left.

Chapter Ten

Benedict stared at the broadsheet's cartoon in the shop window, and stifled a growl. It was horrid. It depicted him with a stern frown standing in between the beautiful Lillian and Beaujolais, with each of them pulling on an arm, with the words '*Mon Duc!*' running beneath the picture. It was ironic, considering neither lady wanted him. He paid for the picture in order to have it removed.

He was still begrudgingly admiring the fair likeness to Beaujolais when Easton caught up with him on the way to the boxing parlour.

"Are you certain you wish to spar with me today? I feel rather like killing someone," Benedict said when he saw his friend.

"I assumed you might. And I assumed a few hits on me would also be welcome," Easton said candidly.

"Ah, so you were involved in the deception," Benedict replied.

"It was not intended to be such. It was hoped you would grow an appreciation for one another and find it humorous when your full identities were discovered. Elly is sick about it."

"Please reassure her on my account. I confess I was angry, but I know you were placed in a precarious position," Benedict added.

"That is handsome of you. When Beaujolais was so adamant in her refusal, we were afraid to tell her you were expected the next day. We hoped she would come to know you as we do," Easton said honestly.

"I am much obliged. I did not realise she was your cousin, of course, or I would have approached you first in the matter."

The men entered the saloon, and stripped to their breeches and donned padded gloves. Once they were sparring and had vented a few punches,

Easton brought up the forbidden.

"Did you speak with Lillian?"

Easton received a crushing right to his abdomen for his efforts.

"I did not."

"Bad luck, that. Who could have known Jolie would invite the one person…"

This time Easton blocked the forceful blow.

"I plan to leave town. I know what is coming, and I do not intend to be the brunt of the *ton's* amusement again."

"It is a shame the gossip columns adore you," Easton agreed sardonically. "However will you find a wife from the country?"

"I have decided my title will have to revert. It is not worth it."

"Perhaps you should consider matters longer," Easton suggested.

"The wounds are reopened, Adam. A wise man knows when to cry off."

"Would you consider a small house party? Elly and I discussed the situation last night, and think it might be best to return to Wyndham with Father. He insists on being here for Livvy. We will invite some of the eligible parties, and you can remove from Lillian."

Benedict pondered a few minutes before answering after they had both stopped to catch their breath.

"Charlotte would prefer it," he admitted. "But how would your cousin feel?"

"Wyndham is large enough for the both of you, and your mother's estate is near should it become unbearable," Easton offered.

"Your cousin also needs to find a match? Or was Hughes mistaken in her eligibility?" Benedict could no longer contain his curiosity.

"She does, though her father will not force her," Easton supplied.

"Admirable. I feel the same about Charlotte. I hope she will fare better than I."

While Benedict was thinking of Beaujolais, however unwillingly, Easton stole a punch.

"Are you growing tired?" Easton teased.

Benedict scoffed. "No, but my mind is constantly distracted by your infuriating cousin," he admitted, pounding his fist into the punching bag.

Easton tried to hide his amusement.

"It is worse now that I know her to be eligible!" Benedict wiped away the sweat dripping down his chin and neck in a furious motion. "I never wanted to feel anything again, Adam. I wanted a business arrangement, and nothing more."

"You picked the wrong lady." Easton confirmed what he already knew.

"It is my gift," Benedict said mockingly.

Easton threw a towel at him, and the lackey handed them both drinks.

"There is one positive," Benedict added.

"What is that?"

"I felt nothing for Lillian when I saw her this time, which is more than I could have ever hoped for."

"I am relieved to know there is a positive side," Easton remarked.

The men washed and dressed, before walking down Bond Street to their residences.

"I will send word as soon as arrangements have been made. Have Hughes send over a list of your prospects whom you wish to receive an invitation."

"I imagine they will all suddenly be otherwise occupied," Benedict said candidly.

"You believe Lillian's resurrection will harm your efforts?" Easton asked, with a thoughtful frown.

"It certainly will not help. It was caricatured in a broadsheet this morning. Would you want to ally yourself with the cold, reclusive, villainous duke?"

Easton gave him a reproachful look. "I collect that is rhetorical?"

Benedict waved his hand dismissively. "I do not know how I always come to be at fault, when it was Lillian who strayed. But people will believe what they wish."

Easton sighed. "Perhaps leaving is for the best. I do not generally advocate for running away from a problem, but I have never been the focus of the *ton's* wrath. You cannot undo the past. Had you stayed, they would have grown bored with you in a fortnight."

"Instead, I am now the circus act," Benedict acknowledged.

Easton stopped. They had come to the point where their paths diverged.

"Speak of the devil!" Easton inclined his head to a shop on the corner, where Lillian stood talking with Lord Dannon.

"I thought Dannon was exiled several years ago, after the incident with Lady Fairmont?"

"He was. He had best hope Loring or Fairmont does not discover his presence in England," Easton said with distaste. Lord Dannon had abused Lady Fairmont when she was his ward, the details of which were not well known—even to Easton. Dannon was also one of the men said to have cuckolded Yardley with Lillian.

"What do you mean to do?" Easton asked, warily searching his friend's face.

"Pay her to leave. I have no delusions she has suddenly acquired a renewed affection for me."

~*~

Benedict sent Easton on his way, despite his friend's offer to stay and support him. Whatever Lillian wanted from him, he desired to face it alone and thus complete the business as soon as possible. She looked up and made eye contact with him. She quickly disengaged from her conversation with Dannon and came towards him, confirming his suspicions she had returned to London for money. He had not moved from where he had left Easton. Determined to remain aloof, he waited for her to approach. He had wasted more than a decade letting her affect him.

"Bonjour, Benedict," she said in the sweet manner that had once enraptured him.

"Renewing old acquaintances?" he asked, referring to her association with Dannon years prior. "You had best remind your lover there is a bounty on his head in England."

"Do you intend to kill him also?" she returned.

"If you expect me to welcome your reappearance with pleasure, you are mistaken, Lillian. Why are you back? What do you want?"

"So blunt and unpleasant," she reproved with the click of her tongue.

"I was not always so," he said with quiet menace.

"I had hoped we could turn over a new leaf, as you say." She gestured with a flutter of her hand.

"I would say, you have already turned over enough leaves in England," he rejoined.

Unruffled, she smiled. "Tut, tut. It is not healthy to bear a grudge. Can you not forgive and forget?" She leaned forward and put her hand on his arm. He stiffened.

"It is not healthy to continue relationships that are poisonous. I allow our past as little thought as possible, which was blissfully little until last evening. You would not be here if you did not want something. Please cut line and tell me what it is."

"Very well, I will leave you alone for ten thousand pounds and my own house in town."

Benedict was quietly considering the ramifications of such an agreement. He crossed his arms and rocked back on his heels a time or two, all the while staring at her coldly.

"With conditions," he finally agreed.

She raised an arrogant eyebrow.

"You will be required to sign an agreement to leave England and never return. An amount will be paid to you through a bank in France, at intervals of twice yearly for ten years, and I will purchase you a home in Paris."

She stood silent but fuming. Her cheeks flushed and her eyes were shooting daggers at him.

"Is that inconvenient, Lillian? It was not convenient for me to have married a whore for a wife, nor go through a public divorce. That is my final offer. You may send word to my solicitor by the end of the week."

He swept a mocking bow and strode away. He cringed inwardly when he heard her begin to scream French profanities at him, but he resisted the urge to turn back and strangle her with his bare hands.

He considered sketching the scene as a cartoon himself and posting it in the broadsheets. Some variation of it was likely to appear anyway, and he ought to at least have the therapeutic benefit of drawing it.

~*~

"How do you think Jolie will react to the news?" Easton asked his wife as they stole a few minutes of quiet in the parlour before tea.

"I do not know. She was trying to disguise her hurt last night. I cannot blame her. It was a gamble and we lost," Elly said remorsefully.

"I still think they are well suited," Easton mused.

"Did I hear you correctly?" Elly looked at her husband in suspicion.

"I did just spend the better part of the afternoon with Benny," he pointed out.

"Then tell me before everyone comes down to tea!" she demanded.

"I will not speak for him, but it is my impression he is fascinated with her."

"I suspect she was unaware of his charms when she refused him. Did you see her watching him?" Elly asked.

"There may be hope yet," Easton agreed.

"Hope for what?" Jolie asked as she entered the room.

"I have a promising filly running at Epsom," Easton replied without blinking.

"Is it Virginia? I would love to watch her race."

"Indeed it is. Perhaps we might attend."

"Jolie, before everyone else comes down, we wanted to apologise. We made a bad decision about Yardley."

"I do understand. Truly. I wish I could say I was unaffected. I think perhaps I am melancholic without my sisters and my parents." She sat dejectedly on the arm of a chair.

"Would you be terribly disappointed if we returned to Wyndham?" Easton asked. "My father is not well, but he refuses to leave whilst Olivia is here."

"Of course not! I do not doubt he suffers in the city air. Please do not think of me. I only wish for my uncle's comfort," she replied graciously.

"You are very good. We would like to invite some of Olivia's friends and potential suitors along for a small house party, if you've no objection." Easton and Elly glanced at each other. "I will tell you that Yardley will be bringing Lady Charlotte. You might imagine he wishes to remove from the gossip. He assures me he will not renew any unwelcome offers."

"He agreed to this?" Jolie asked, astonished.

Easton inclined his head.

"Who am I to say nay? We are all adults and can behave," she responded.

"Thank you for your understanding, Jolie. We would have honoured your wishes if you were uncomfortable. Yardley can remove to his mother's estate should you desire."

"It is not my place to determine your guests. I shall not mind his presence."

"Do you have any thoughts on eligible gentlemen whom we might invite, to further acquaintance for Olivia and Charlotte and perhaps, yourself?" Elly asked.

"I have little interest, I'm afraid. Invite whom you see fit. I will say Captain Harris danced twice with Olivia and seems taken with her."

"I know him to be honourable. I will speak to Olivia," Easton said.

"We could invite Summers if you like," Elly teased.

Jolie made a playful face, rising to greet the children as they entered for tea.

"I have had a letter from a friend in Scotland, and he mentions Margaux," Easton recalled.

"Is she well? I expected a letter by this time, but it might have been directed to Sussex."

"He said she is helping with his children until the governess arrives."

"I suppose that is what she wanted. I still believe *Maman* will bring her back before autumn."

"If you wish to send a letter, we are sending some of the veterans to work at a nearby estate. They leave first thing on the morrow," he added.

"I shall see to it at once. Thank you."

Dearest Sister,

So much has happened since you left, I do not know where to begin. No, I am not betrothed, nor am I likely to be soon. Easton and Elly decided to bring Olivia out early since my uncle is ill and they do not think his heart is strong enough to last until next Season. In fact, we had a coming-out party for Olivia and Lady Charlotte, but are soon to return to Sussex with a small house party, to be with him. The Duke of Yardley will be present since he is a long-time friend of Easton's, but do not put your hopes in that quarter for me. However, he is not as disagreeable as you imagined him to be.

There is no word from Anjou, but none was to be expected this soon.

How do you enjoy spinsterhood? It appears I may soon be enjoying it with you.

Ever yours,
Jolie

Chapter Eleven

This is worse than Almack's, Benedict thought to himself as he gazed around the drawing room in horror. In addition to his sister, there were three other young ladies and three young men present. He thought he might as well be in the nursery, for all the difference in their ages. A hush fell over the room when he entered, and he strode towards his sister with his ingrained ducal confidence.

"Good morning, Charlotte, Lady Olivia," he said, assuming the formal manner he reverted to when on display.

He was struggling to recall the names of the other two ladies, though he had danced with them at Easton's party.

"Lady Anna." He bowed to the tall brunette with tight ringlets framing a thin face, as he pulled her name from his distracted memories of that tumultuous evening only a few days prior.

"Miss Breton." He bowed to the average miss with the average face, average figure, and average hair—not altogether unpleasing.

One family had declined the invitation after the return of Lillian and the ensuing scandal, so there were even fewer Eligibles at this house party.

He felt the young ladies' eyes evaluating him as he had done them, though he had done it with the subtle skill of a man seasoned. He neither felt anything, nor cared what they thought of him. It was promising. If he could but determine one of them could live companionably long enough to breed heirs, he would be satisfied.

"Would you mind leading us on an expedition to Brighton? Easton is tied up in business helping our old friend Dr Craig finding some workers to send to Scotland, and then Easton and Elly are off to the Abbey," Olivia asked of him.

He would like nothing less than to go to Brighton, but he swallowed his protests.

"I have no objection if we are to ride," he answered.

He heard a gasp from Lady Anna. Was she to be struck from the list so soon? He did not think he could tolerate anyone who had an aversion to horses or riding. Not that he intended to spend much time riding with his new wife, he conjectured.

"We can also take the curricle if you do not ride. The path can accommodate a small vehicle. I am certain one of the gentleman would be pleased to show off his handiness with the ribbons." Olivia said, looking pleadingly at the men as she attempted to placate Lady Anna.

Sir Percival was happy to rescue a damsel in distress with a charming dowry. It was amusing to compare the crop of men with the ladies. The former were all in dire need of funds or heirs, and the latter had generous allotments and were of noble birth. It was the dream of all matchmakers.

Benedict glanced towards Miss Breton, who was the daughter of Viscount Redding, and a school friend of Charlotte and Olivia. Charlotte had at one time confessed an admiration for Miss Breton's cleverness and wit. He would try to engage her in some conversation on the ride, if she could keep up. He had no intention of trotting at a sedate pace.

And then the moment of hope was lost. Lady Beaujolais entered the room.

The gentleman rose to their feet.

"Jolie!" Olivia exclaimed. "We were organising a ride to Brighton. Please say you will join us!"

Benedict groaned inwardly.

Beaujolais made a quick scan of the room and smiled. "Good morning to you all." She looked down and indicated her violet-hued riding habit. "I was already planning to ride. I'm trying one of Easton's fast-goers today, so if any of you think you can keep up, I am sure it would be pleasant to ride to Brighton and back," she said provocatively.

"That, gentleman, sounds like a wager!" Sir Percival said enthusiastically.

"I would not bet against Lady Beaujolais," Yardley warned.

She looked at the men and tutted. "I do not think a race is quite what the ladies had in mind for their expedition. However, I do intend to let the horse at its paces."

"Shall we change into our riding attire and meet at the stables?" Olivia stood and smiled at the group before any bets could be placed.

~*~

Jolie made her way to the stables to request horses for the outing, needing to remove herself from the gathering since Easton was not there to do so. She was not certain the house was large enough for herself and Yardley. She had been hoping for a ride with Mr Stanton before she knew he was Yardley. She suspected he was a bruising rider and she would enjoy it very much. She struck her crop against her boot in a rare outburst of frustration when she knew she would not be witnessed. She also knew this house party was to facilitate matches, but she had little interest in any of the gentleman. None of them held a candle to Yardley. Despite everything, she could not keep him from her thoughts.

The head groom, Jensen, came to assist her as she examined the horses.

"I would leave Hector for his Grace. Unless you think he might prefer his own mount." She realised she was being presumptuous. She was to ride on Alexandria today, and would enjoy watching Yardley master Hector.

"Aye, t'would be the only other person Master Adam would trust wi' 'im," the older groom remarked. "He's right devilish today. 'e could use a good ride."

"Is he displeased with Dido?"

"Oh, no. 'Tis 'er who doesn't want 'im," Jensen surmised as they continued to survey the mounts.

Olivia had her own filly, as did Charlotte from Yardley's prized stables.

Jolie selected a mare for Miss Breton and geldings for Captain Harris and Mr Beaumont, since they had arrived by carriage. There was no bad stock to choose from here. The grooms set to saddling the horses, and she made her way over to Alexandria to become acquainted. The mare was a lean, silky chestnut Arabian with powerful legs. She was not as large as Hector, but Jolie knew she would test her skill.

"Greetings, my fair Alexandria."

The horse looked up and took a moment to assess her.

"Very discerning, are you?" Jolie held out her hand to greet the mare, which walked proudly to her and sniffed her. She stood on a stool to reach her mane and stroke it.

"She be a fresh one, but 'er'll give ye a good ride if'n 'er is pleased wi' ye," Jensen opined.

"I will credit her with excellent taste," Jolie said with a playful smile.

Yardley approached and her smile straightened. She looked back to the horse.

"Will yer Grace be riding yer own or one of 'is lordship's? 'Er ladyship thought you'd enjoy riding Hector today. He needs it," Jensen warned.

"It would be my pleasure to ride Hector, Jensen. Perhaps he can keep up with Alexandria," he replied, tossing Jolie's words back at her yet again. She refused to turn around. She would make certain she was not forced into his company all day. She was too old to play this game any longer, she reflected as she watched the younger set approach. The marriage mart and its flirtations were palling after five years. She felt ancient when she watched them and their zest for silliness. What had changed? She could hardly credit her melancholy solely to her disappointment in Yardley; likely her parents and sisters being absent was also responsible in part. She longed to be alone. But she was not about to let on she was anything but delighted with her current situation in life. She would act merry if it killed her.

Sir Percival, in a dashing waistcoat of navy blue and puce stripes, escorted Lady Anna on his arm. It appeared he was successfully coaxing a smile from the nervous girl as he twirled her parasol about. He was all that was ridiculous, but his nature was excellent.

Lady Charlotte was behind them. Jolie had yet to have any conversation with Yardley's sister. She was no longer certain the acquaintance would be welcome. From her observations, the girl appeared haughty. However, some people thought Anjou aloof, but she was simply shy around large groups of people. Jolie would try to bear that in mind. Lady Charlotte was full-figured, but many a lady used that to her advantage. Jolie walked at a distance from Mr Beaumont and Miss Breton, who appeared to be having a one-sided conversation. Elly had mentioned he was self-made, heavily involved in business in India and looking for a genteel match.

Captain Harris followed behind with Olivia. He was dashing in or out of uniform, as he was for the ride. They made a splendid pair; Jolie wondered if there was anything more than friendship brewing between the two. He was the only other person with more than thirty years under his belt in the group, save Yardley, and she wondered if Harris felt it as keenly as she did. She was certain Yardley did, by the look on his face.

"I never imagined we would be forced into the chaperone role," Yardley said, moving right behind her as they watched the couples grow closer.

"We are certainly old enough," she countered.

He harrumphed in an elegant way. "And you have reached the elderly age of what, four-and-twenty?"

"Are we acquainted again? I recall quite clearly having heard you mention we were not." *Did I say that out loud? He is making me into a tyrant!* Jolie thought to herself.

"I beg your pardon. Again." He bowed curtly and walked away to examine horses and begin discussing Hector's merits with Jensen.

The others approved of their mounts and were aided into their saddles with the help of a mounting block and grooms. Sir Percival and Lady Anna were waiting nearby in the curricle.

"Lead the way, Lady Charlotte. Shall we all pause at Rottingdean and meet up so we can all ride at our favoured paces?" Olivia suggested.

"That is a dashed good notion," Sir Percival said obligingly.

Thus agreed, the group set off on their mounts.

When Jolie mounted and began to walk Alexandria, she noticed the mare was favouring her right side. She immediately jumped down from the horse to examine her. The groom had also noticed and was running over.

"I do not think she is fit to ride, Jensen. She seems to have an injured hock."

"I canna'e tell ye 'ow this 'appened."

"No matter. We can saddle another."

Jensen whistled. "There be no more prime goers in the stables. The other ladies and gennelmen be mounted on 'em."

Jolie bit back her frustration. "Who do you have that is rideable? My cousin has no poor horses."

"Other'n the children's ponies, the only one is Dido. Lord and Lady Easton 'ave ridden over to Loring Abbey this morning."

"Dido? His Grace's Dido?" she asked with surprise, while her thoughts took on a devious tone.

"Yes, m'lady," he said with a frown.

"Saddle her," she commanded.

"I do not think...," he started to say doubtfully, but then he grinned. "Yes, m'lady."

Yardley would probably have a heart spasm. Or wring her neck, if he could catch her.

The groom soon had her saddle on Dido, and boosted her into the seat.

"Mayhap a good ride'll soften 'er..."

"I'll convince her of his charms," she assured him with a smile as she led Dido away.

She was several minutes behind the others, and she wanted to be careful the mare was unharmed. She also wanted to consider how to handle Yardley. If he was near the others he was less likely to thrash her. Her blood began to pound in anticipation of the look on his face. She grinned and leaned forward for flight.

Dido ran like the wind. She was divine, and Jolie soon forgot about everything but the moment. She did not notice she was approaching the group of riders until she was upon them. She did not wish to stop so she tipped her hat and winked at Yardley as she flew past, even though it was not good form.

"By George!" Sir Percival said appreciatively.

"Was that Dido?" Lady Charlotte asked.

Yardley did not answer, but Jolie heard him urge Hector forward.

When she realised he was close on her heels, she urged Dido on.

Then he did the unthinkable. He whistled to his mare and Dido stopped, almost throwing Jolie. He grabbed the bridle.

"How dare you!"

"How dare I? Is that not my horse?"

"You know you could have injured her, not to mention myself, with a stunt like that!"

"She is well trained. Would you like to explain why you are riding her?"

"Not particularly," she said defiantly.

He glared at her.

"Very well. Alexandria had an injured hock and there were no other mounts available."

He said nothing.

Jolie dismounted and began to walk off.

"Where are you going?"

"If I mean to make Wyndham by dark I had best start now," she said angrily over her shoulder. "Enjoy Brighton!"

The Duke growled. "Very well. You may ride her." He dismounted and walked after her.

"No, thank you."

"Enough! I was surprised. You will not walk back," he insisted.

She kept walking.

He followed angrily, leading the horses, who were causing a commotion of their own. Hector was becoming overly friendly with Dido and she was voicing her displeasure. Jolie saw the Duke attempting to manage Hector's *amour* and burst out laughing.

"Would you care to take one of them?" he asked sarcastically.

"Oh, I do not think so. I have not been so entertained in some time."

"Please," he growled as he struggled with them.

"I thought the aim was to breed them?" she rejoined.

He let go of the horses, then picked Jolie up by the waist and placed her on Dido.

Jolie was too shocked to speak.

He patted Dido on the rump and she trotted away from Hector.

Jolie rode by herself the remainder of the way to Rottingdean, although she could hear the curricle's wheels rattling not far behind. She left the Duke in a foul mood, and she wished herself anywhere but there. The horses took a quick drink from a stream near the path, and they proceeded to Brighton, which was thankfully not much further.

A picnic lunch had been arranged for them at a park near the Pavilion. Jolie sat near Olivia and Captain Harris, while Yardley chose to sit with his sister and Mr Beaumont. Jolie refused to make eye contact, intently examining her glass of mulberry wine and picking at her food.

"I thought that was a dashed funny game, Jolie riding past on Dido," Sir Percival remarked.

Yardley still did not appear to see the humour by the perpetual scowl he wore.

"Benny has lost his sense of humour," Lady Charlotte remarked. "Years ago he would have been laughing with the rest of us and calling her a great gun."

Sir Percival smacked Yardley on the back jovially, which loosened the frown a bit.

"I think it was scandalous to take a horse without permission and then to flaunt it right in front of all of us, no less," Lady Anna said with a disapproving frown.

"She did not steal the horse. If we had been more considerate, we would have waited for her before riding away," Captain Harris said tactfully.

Jolie would have preferred to hide at the moment, but her bonnet was shockingly small.

Lady Olivia quickly attempted to divert the conversation to safer waters. "Captain Harris, you mentioned you had a brother. Is he also a sailor?"

"He is, in fact, I believe your sister and brother are now on board my brother's ship to America," he said to Jolie.

She perked up at news of her sister. "If you hear anything, I would love to be apprised," she said gratefully.

"I will be happy to relay a message. If we are fortunate, we will hear within another week or two. Edward sends word back upon his arrival if he is not returning immediately."

"I do not like waiting. I have a new respect for the wives of sailors. It must be a difficult lot," she said thoughtfully.

"It can be. All are not fortunate enough to be able to take family with them. And those wives who do go are not faint of heart," he said casting a quick glance at Olivia and then away again.

"I think it would be interesting to see other lands," Miss Breton remarked.

"You should see India one day," Mr Beaumont chimed in. "It is an entirely different world from this one, with strange flavours and spices, peculiar music and language, vibrant colours and plants..." He trailed off.

"You make it sound romantic," Miss Breton said dreamily.

"I suppose in some ways it is," he said thoughtfully.

"You may find all of those things in Prinny's Pavilion, including the heat. But seeing as we do not have an invitation, we will have to delay our foray into the exotic," Sir Percival remarked in a bantering tone, describing the Prince Regent's opulent Pavilion filled with ornamentation from eastern lands.

The wind was picking up and some clouds were rolling in from the Channel, and blew Mr Beaumont's hat off.

"I think we had best head back soon as it appears there is a storm brewing," Lady Anna said anxiously.

"That is probably wise," Sir Percival agreed.

"We can probably make it to Langdon House before the rain," Lady Charlotte suggested.

"That is an excellent idea," Captain Harris agreed.

"Then it is settled," Sir Percival announced.

Jolie had no intention of stopping anywhere. As they gathered their things, she whispered to Olivia and went to the horses the grooms had brought back to them.

"Is that Lillian?" Lady Charlotte asked in disbelief as Yardley's former wife strolled openly along the street on the arm of Lord Dannon.

"Good God," Yardley muttered under his breath.

Jolie felt a little sorry for him.

"She's coming this way," Olivia said in disbelief. "Are we supposed to cut her?"

"She will not notice if you do," he said inaudibly.

"What does she want, Benedict?" Charlotte asked.

"Money, of course."

"Can you not make her leave?"

"Would that I could," he muttered. "Go on ahead, I will catch up directly."

Jolie and the group walked away to mount the horses, while Yardley stood, looking angry as Lillian and Dannon approached him.

"Good afternoon, Benedict. Lovely day for a stroll, *non*? Are they hurrying away because of me?" Lillian asked innocently, twirling a loose curl seductively.

"Have you decided to reject my offer?" he asked impatiently.

"Let us say a better offer has taken precedence." She pulled Lord Dannon closer with a smug smile.

Benedict raised a condescending brow, but said nothing.

"Much better than working, *non*?" Lillian cooed.

"As long as you realise yet another lover will likely not live to see your next day of birth once Loring and Fairmont discover his presence in England, which I believe was made known to them this morning."

"They have no right to deny me my own country when the Prince Regent has no objection," Lord Dannon said self-righteously.

"It is not my battle to fight, nor one I would sully my hands over," Benedict sneered.

"It is too late for that, *cherie*," Lillian cackled as he walked away to where the groom was waiting with Hector. Benedict mounted and rode in the most nonchalant manor he could manage, until he was out of the town and could allow his anger to ease with a more bruising gallop. He was back at Langdon before he was ready to stop, but drops of rain were pattering on his coat, and the sounds of thunder were not far in the distance. He entered the gates to his mother's seaside abode and rode straight to the stables to check on Dido, but when he looked she was nowhere to be found.

Chapter Twelve

"Where the devil is she?" Benedict demanded as he stormed into the drawing room in his muddy boots, gripping his crop. He was met with shocked stares from everyone in the party except the one he was looking for.

"What is the matter, Benedict?" his sister asked, frowning at his dirty state.

"Are you looking for Lady Beaujolais?" Olivia asked.

"More specifically, my horse!" he fumed. "I assume I will find one with the other."

"She rode on back to Wyndham. Said she was not feeling quite the thing," Sir Percival replied.

"And you let her go alone?"

Sir Percival swallowed quietly and nodded.

Benedict closed his eyes. He was going to strangle the woman when he found her. He turned on his heel and marched back to the stables. The groom's eyes grew wide when he called for Hector again and then proceeded to mount him and ride away.

"Of course, it was all this day lacked," he murmured to himself, as a pop of thunder sounded and the heavens opened up. He urged Hector forward to make as much time as possible before the roads became impassable. The rain was beating so hard against his face, with the water pouring around his hat, that he could not see the way. He veered Hector as far to the left of the path as he could and slowed him to a walk.

"A sane man would find shelter," he chastised himself. "She is addling my attics."

All of a sudden, Hector veered off the path straight across a marshy valley. "Are you overruling me, old boy?"

Benedict allowed the stallion to lead, and when he could see, he found what had drawn him off the road, he held his tongue. Lady Beaujolais and Dido were seeking shelter under an old oak. Benedict almost forgave her when he saw how drenched her habit and hair were. However, when he recalled he was in a similar state, he thought better of it.

"Apparently Hector would also be an excellent hound," he remarked.

"How kind for you to be concerned for me," she retorted.

"You are riding my horse," he pointed out.

"Ah, I should have known your concern is only for the beast. As you can see, she is unharmed. Being a poor horsewoman is one thing I have never been accused of, at least."

"Risking my horse in this storm does little to recommend your judgement, however."

"Spoken from the mouth of an expert," she countered.

He clenched his jaw and held back a riposte.

"Shall we cry truce? At least until we depart Wyndham? It appears we are to be forced together and we might as well attempt civility."

"Am I being uncivil?" she asked as Hector began to nudge Dido.

Benedict firmly pulled back on the bit to remind Hector to behave, but the stubborn horse yawed at the reins. "You will notice I said 'we', and what the deuce is wrong with Hector?"

"I believe Dido is what is wrong, though she is not happy about the notion." The mare's ears were flattened, indicating she was becoming agitated.

The rain began to pour even harder from the sky, and the only way to separate the horses at this point would be to go out into the rain and mud.

Hector pranced about, displaying his wares and nudging Dido.

"Make him stop! I have no wish to be sitting a horse during their, ah, *amour*, thank you," she said, unaccustomed to having to discuss such inappropriate things.

"I suppose you wish me to ride him away in this storm and preferably over a cliff?" he asked sardonically.

Meanwhile, Dido was baring her teeth at Hector.

"She is going to bolt if he does not stop," Jolie said, growing nervous.

"Very well. Hector, our efforts are wasted here," Benedict directed a meaningful glance and pulled on the bit to direct Hector into the storm and urge him forward. But the stallion was not to be so easily deterred. He reared on his hind legs and deposited Benedict into the mud, for it had been too slick to hold on. Before Beaujolais could react, Hector was heading directly for Dido, who, in her aversion to Hector, bolted, and Beaujolais was not expecting it. She lost her seat as well, and found herself also decorated with Sussex mire.

"Where is your whistle now?" Jolie asked. She glared at Benedict as they watched the horses run away.

"Would you return if you were being chased by an unwelcome suitor?"

She narrowed her eyes and attempted to whistle herself, but only managed to spittle. Benedict had to turn his head to control his laughter.

"I do hope she will not injure herself in a rabbit hole," he said watching the mare trying to evade the stallion after he had composed himself.

"Perhaps you should remove her to the Duchess' stables until you return home. That would keep her away from Hector."

He looked back at her as they sat in the muck and scoffed. "Perhaps she is merely pretending to be difficult."

They watched as Hector tried to assert himself. Dido objected to his advances and kicked him in the chest with both hind feet. Clearly hearing the thud, Jolie cast a doubtful glance at Benedict.

The rain was finally slowing, and he saw Jolie attempting to rise from the mud. He hurried to his feet and held out a hand to help her.

She cast a suspicious glance at the hand.

"So I am not even worthy to be a gentleman?"

She cocked an eyebrow, but placed her hand in his. He would not have thought anyone could be attractive with their hair and clothing plastered to them, and at the same time sporting a red nose, but somehow she was.

Lady Beaujolais gathered her skirts above her ankles and began to walk away.

"Where are you going? You do not mean to come between Dido and Hector, surely?"

"I intend nothing of the sort. However, I do not intend to stand in the mud any longer."

"You mean to walk?"

"I do."

Benedict had no better suggestion, and knew not what to do about the horses, so he followed her. As they regained the lane, he looked over to find Hector covering Dido and he erupted into laughter. "By Jove!" he exclaimed.

Lady Beaujolais could not help but look either, and gave out a disgusted, "*Traitre!*"

Brought swiftly to his senses and with an aplomb he did not know he possessed, Benedict reached out to screen her eyes with his hand.

Uttering an unladylike oath, she batted it away.

"I cannot even rely on a mare to stand up for our sex."

Benedict refrained from the retort that was dancing on his tongue. "The good news is, I suspect we will not have to walk the entire way."

She made another noise of disgust and stomped more purposefully along the muddy path.

Some twenty minutes later of walking in silence, the two naughty horses caught up with them after Benedict whistled.

Lady Beaujolais glared at the creatures.

Benedict fought a smile. "Shall I boost you up?"

She gave a reluctant nod. When he put his hands on her waist she was shaking.

He began to strip off his riding cape and wrap it around her. "You are catching cold. Why did you not tell me?"

"I am not sick," she insisted and sneezed for emphasis.

"Are you able to ride? I do not think it is above two more miles."

She urged Dido forward by way of response and he mounted Hector and chased after her. By the time they arrived at Wyndham, Lady Beaujolais' face was burning and she looked ready to fall from the saddle. He pulled her from the horse and into his arms, and carried her into the house asking for Lady Easton, while shaking his head and muttering about stubborn females.

~*~

Jolie awoke to the feeling of cold and wet on her forehead. She opened her eyes.

"How are you feeling? I did not mean to wake you," Elly said while laying a cold cloth across her brow.

"I feel a little tired. Did something happen to me?"

"I believe it is only a little chill," Elly replied. "However, you did swoon in Yardley's arms."

110

"Bother! Of all things," Jolie exclaimed.

Elly smiled. "He was very concerned, if that is any consolation. You slept through a bath and for the remainder of the afternoon. A tray will be here shortly, as it is time for dinner. A letter has arrived from Scotland for you." Elly stood as a maid entered with a tray. "Do ring for me if you need anything."

"Thank you," Jolie replied as Elly and the maid left.

She refused to be sick, so she decided she would join the others after dinner. She made decent work of the gruel and toast on her tray, and eagerly broke open the letter from her family.

Dearest Daughter,

Your sister is most stubborn about remaining in Scotland. Your mother and I have decided to return for the remainder of the Season. I have a notion Margaux will be bored within a fortnight if left alone.

Jolie chuckled. "Very likely," she agreed out loud.

You may expect us within a fortnight from when you receive this, if all goes as planned.

Ever your loving father,

Ashbury

Jolie held the letter to her chest and breathed deeply of her father's scent. How she missed her family! She turned the page to read Margaux's epistle.

Dearest Sister,

Maman *and* Papa *have finally agreed to leave me here at Breconrae with Aunt Ida, who, thankfully, is not much of a chaperone. There is little to occupy me, I confess, but I need to make the best of it. There is a family in need of my assistance until their new governess arrives, and I am certain I will find some new acquaintance in the village shortly.*

I do hope you will visit as I miss you dearly. For now, Scotland's beauty consoles my loneliness.

All my love,

Margaux

Jolie shook her head. Margaux was short and to the point as usual. She still did not understand what had entered into her sister's mind. Of a certainty, she would soon realise her folly and return to her family.

Since Jolie was not attending dinner, she decided to put on a simple muslin dress and leave her hair in a loose knot. She still was not feeling quite the thing. However, she refused to succumb or let Yardley see that she was overly fagged. She made her way downstairs and decided to soothe herself with some Bach while she waited for the others to join her.

"You play well," Lady Charlotte remarked, rather than complimented, as she entered the room.

"Thank you," Jolie replied, looking past Lady Charlotte for the rest of the ladies.

"Oh, they are not quite finished. I made my excuses," she said noticing Jolie's gaze. "My mother," she offered as her only explanation.

Jolie said nothing and continued to finger a tune quietly.

Lady Charlotte took a seat and stared. Jolie did not feel much like conversation, so she resumed her playing until spoken to.

"Are you dangling after my brother?" the girl asked bluntly.

Jolie missed several keys and lost her concentration.

"Forgive me. Mother always says I should not speak plainly, but I've never mastered the art of duplicity. The others have been speculating about you. Benedict pays no notice to any of the other ladies."

"I do not know how to reply to that," Jolie answered. "I neither am, nor am not."

"Are you trying to answer so as not to offend me?" Lady Charlotte asked candidly.

"No, I am simply ambivalent about the situation." Jolie gave a slight nod, and watched her fingers play.

Lady Charlotte laughed approvingly. "I'm deuced glad to hear it," she said using language fit for the stables, not for a drawing room. "You would not believe the ladies who have toad-eaten me to be near him recently. When they said you were on the hunt for a duke, I confess I have avoided you. But I have also watched you, and if you are casting lures, I'll eat my hat."

"Ah. The sentiment was a childhood jest amongst my family. Your brother is safe from my arrows."

"It matters not to me as long as he is treated well. I may have been young, but I saw what Lillian did to him," she said in a mournful tone.

"And continues to do," Jolie remarked.

"I trust Lillian will leave him be once he remarries. She wants his money and power."

"She has an odd way of showing it, on the arm of another man," Jolie retorted.

"She is hoping Benedict will be jealous as he was before, but Benedict will not be fooled twice. I will wring his neck, first."

"She is very beautiful," Jolie reasoned with the girl.

"Not once you know her. Besides, I've seen him watching you," Lady

Charlotte argued.

The others entered the room before Jolie had time to reply. She wanted to retire and consider Lady Charlotte's words, but Yardley was walking towards her.

"Lady Beaujolais, are you recovered?" he asked.

The genuine concern on his face made her heart skip a beat.

"It was only a slight chill," she said dismissively, and looked down at her fingers as they caressed the keys.

"I am delighted to hear it."

"Are you going to play for us?" Sir Percival asked her.

"You must not feel obligated if you do not feel well enough," Yardley said with concern.

"I believe I can manage a song. Do you have a particular request?"

"Are you familiar with Beethoven's new Sonata?" Benedict surprised her by saying.

"Very little. It is a most challenging piece. I could not play it from memory."

"I have the music should you care to attempt it." Elly retrieved the sheets from a bureau and handed them to Yardley.

"How convenient," Jolie murmured, since sheet music was difficult to come by.

She began to play the Sonata No. 29, but Yardley stood close by and turned the sheets for her. It was unsettling, and she found herself having difficulty concentrating and playing the right notes. It was an exhausting piece under normal circumstances. When at last she finished the final movement, she turned to Yardley as everyone applauded appreciatively.

"Elly tells me I owe you my gratitude for your help earlier. I confess, I do not remember your heroism."

"No gratitude is required. I must admit that it was a pleasure to help you without any objection," he said with a twinkle in his eyes that belied his words. "Shall we play cards with the others?"

Jolie looked at the groups gathering for cards and there were two of extremes: a younger and an older.

"I am not certain my mind is sharp enough tonight." She made an excuse, though if truth be told, the Sonata had taken the little energy she had.

"Then, unless that is your way of fobbing me off, would you care to stroll through the garden now that the rain has passed?"

"How could I refuse?" she asked, not masking the sardonic tone in her voice.

"It has not stopped you previously," he said with a rare half-smile which displayed a charming dimple.

She laughed and took his arm. "If I did not frighten you away this afternoon, then far be it for me to resist."

He chose the garden facing the sea, and the sun was painting a glorious array of pinks and lavenders across the horizon. It would have been romantic in any other situation. He stayed near to the terrace doors, and led her to a bench.

"Your marriage plans will not be furthered by escaping the festivities," she pointed out.

"I have already made my choice," he said, throwing Jolie off.

"I'm happy to hear it. When shall the blessed announcement be made?" she asked, trying to stifle the inexplicable urge to cry.

"I will leave those details to the bride when I ask her."

She nodded absently. "I'm glad to know you mean to ask." She could not resist the barb.

"I am a quick study," he responded drily.

"I am happy to have been useful to you then," she said with a forced smile. "Will you be leaving us soon, then?"

"I suppose that is dependent on my sister," he replied.

"Ah, yes. The charming Lady Charlotte."

He laughed and his face changed. "Forgive me, but charming and Charlotte are not words I have ever heard used simultaneously."

"I even used them in one sentence. She is direct and odd, but I found I rather liked her. So, yes, charming."

"I am pleased to hear it," he said, his tone genuine.

Jolie stood. "I beg you will forgive me, but I find I am rather more fatigued than I anticipated."

"Of course. Is there anything I can do for you?" he asked, as he moved to help her.

"This is nothing that sleep cannot cure," she reassured him.

"Good night then, Lady Beaujolais."

"Good night. And do, please, call me Jolie. I believe our adventures today put us past formalities."

"Indeed." He gave an acknowledging nod as she walked back into the drawing room.

~*~

Benedict made his way into the drawing room some few minutes later, after taking some time to reflect. Had he imagined disappointment in her face when he told her he had chosen a bride? He did not think she would accept him yet, but he might wear her down some day. She had seemed almost friendly to him tonight.

He would have to thank Easton for bringing them back to Wyndham. He and Jolie had been thrown together often here, which was only natural since the younger set were finding more amusement together.

He must have been outside longer than he thought, for the drawing room was deserted and the servants were tidying up. He walked on through to Easton's study, where Lord Fairmont and Easton were discussing Lord Dannon.

"The others have gone to bed?" Benedict asked as he strolled to an armchair and sat down.

"They retired with Jolie. It was a tiring day, I hear," Easton said.

"It is true, then?" Lord Fairmont asked.

"About Dannon and Lillian?" Benedict queried as he examined his nails. "They are back in the country, strolling around like besotted puppies and trying to extort money from me, if that is to what you refer."

Fairmont slammed his glass down on the desk. "Why are you not as angry as I?"

"I suppose because I am the one Lillian hurt, whereas Dannon hurt someone you love. Not to mention that I have been angry for over a decade."

Fairmont reddened and he sat back down. "I beg your pardon. I, of all people, have no right to accuse anyone of indifference. But I refuse to sit complacently while they stroll about and he is allowed to hurt more innocent victims."

"Lillian is hardly innocent," Benedict reminded his friends.

"Persons of his mettle move on when they tire of their game. I will never be the one to say people cannot change, but they appear to be up to trickery."

"What can we do about it? Lillian refused my generous offer, Dannon has Prinny on his side, and murder is not as rewarding as one might think."

"We can make life extremely uncomfortable for them," Fairmont suggested.

"That would assume they either have a conscience or care. They are already cut in polite circles."

"I refer to finding a way to cut off his funds," Fairmont said. "Prinny will have little use for Dannon if he is poor. My father, you, Easton, and I—four of the wealthiest peers in the kingdom—can find a way to make him wish he were dead, or at least very uncomfortable."

"Lillian would at least move on to greener pastures," Benedict agreed. "Tell me what you need of me. Hughes is rather astute at investigating matters. He can be at your disposal."

"Excellent. I have a strong suspicion there is more to Dannon and Lillian's re-emergence than meets the eye."

Chapter Thirteen

Benedict walked absent-mindedly toward his rooms, pondering
Lillian's behaviour in Brighton. He was afraid to be hopeful that
Fairmont would find anything useful in order to remove her from his
sphere. He had no idea why she had emerged after a decade, and when
he was prepared to remarry, no less. He was too tired to contemplate
anything further following the day's festivities, and climbed into bed as
soon as he had dismissed his valet.

Within seconds, it seemed, he bolted upright when a scream rent the
air. Throwing off the covers, his heart pounding, he ran to the sound. It
came from a room further along the corridor from his own. Reaching the
door he heard weeping, and he thrust it open before his rational self
stopped to think better of it.

Beaujolais was tossing and turning in her bed, while at the same time
crying out.

"Save her! Margaux, no!"

He ran to her side and awkwardly attempted to comfort her by patting
her arm. "Wake up, Beaujolais. You are having a bad dream."

"You must help her!" she insisted, grabbing his arm.

"Help whom?" He sat down on the side of the bed.

"My sister. Save her!" She was shaking his arms to emphasise her
desperation.

She leaned her head on his shoulder and began to cry.

"Shh," he murmured in her ear and stroked her hair.

"I must go to her," she cried.

"Of course. Everything will be better in the morning."

She shook her head violently in denial. "No. I feel things. We all do when it happens to each other."

"Is she running a fever?" Elly asked from behind him, causing him to jump. "I heard her scream."

"I have no notion of those things," he replied.

Elly put down her candle and felt of her forehead. "Perhaps a mild fever."

Jolie grabbed her arm. "I must go to her! She needs me!"

"We cannot go in the middle of the night," Elly placated the distraught girl. She turned to Benedict. "I will go for a fever powder. Will you stay with her?"

"Of course," he replied. Though he soon wondered if it was he who was insane when Jolie jumped from the bed in her nightgown and began to furiously pack her things.

"Beaujolais, you should go back to bed. You had a nightmare, is all. Everything will be fine come morning. Elly went to fetch you a fever powder."

"Do not patronise me," she said and pulled away from his arms as he attempted to lead her back to bed.

He held up his hands in surrender and found a nearby chair to sit in until Elly returned. He enjoyed watching Jolie's fury more than he should have. If anyone else were to walk in, they would be shackled for life. That he fully intended to happen, but in his own way—with a willing bride.

Elly returned and gave him a look of reprimand, but he merely shrugged his shoulders. Who was he to interfere with this force of nature? Besides, he knew not if Jolie was awake, delirious or sleepwalking.

"Jolie." Elly attempted to stop her to give her the medicine. "Jolie!" she said louder, shaking her, but Jolie would not be deterred from her task.

Elly reached for the nearby pitcher of water and proceeded to dump its contents on Jolie.

Jolie gasped with shock, and Benedict stood abruptly to leave. "That is my cue."

He walked out of the room while deliberately forcing himself to look away. He went back down to the study knowing there would be little sleep for him that night, wishing he could be there to comfort her.

~*~

"Why did you do that?" Jolie asked. She looked confused.

"You were sleepwalking and I needed to give you a fever powder. You had a nightmare."

"I do not need a fever powder," Jolie insisted.

"Are you telling me you have been awake the whole time?" Elly asked with disbelief as she retrieved a dry gown from the bureau and handed it to Jolie.

"I do not know. I had that feeling. Something is wrong with Margaux. I know it. I must go to her," she said. She lifted her arms as Elly helped out of the soaked gown and into the dry one.

"You cannot just go to her in Scotland," Elly reasoned gently.

"I can travel post with my maid."

"No, you cannot. Try to get some sleep," Elly said, stifling a yawn.

"Elly, it was not just a bad dream!"

"Whatever it is, you cannot leave tonight. If you still feel you must leave in the morning, Adam and I will think of a way. Adam and I cannot leave with the Earl so ill."

"I know. I am sorry to be so much trouble. But you know the bond my sisters and I have. I cannot explain it but I feel something is wrong."

"I cannot know exactly, but I know my children have a similar feeling," Elly said sympathetically.

"I realise it seems unreasonable and irrational."

Elly stepped towards her and put her arm around her for comfort.

"Take this powder and try to sleep. If you mean to go, you must be strong. However, I refuse to let you go without a chaperone."

Jolie nodded and drank the medicine with a grimace.

"Yes, it tastes horrid," Elly agreed. "Good night, and I will try to think of someone who could help you." She tucked Jolie into bed as she would one of her own children.

"Thank you, Elly," she said. As the door closed, she turned on to her side and wept quiet, harrowing tears until exhaustion at last claimed her, and sleep.

~*~

Benedict had wandered up to his bed after several hours in the study and a glass or two of wine. He had attempted sleep, but had tossed and turned. He now sat alone in the breakfast room on his fourth cup of coffee, while mulling over the latest paper and note from his secretary. As he had anticipated, the gossip columns were full of Lillian's return and speculation about her intentions. He angrily took a bite out of his toast.

"You look like you have not slept," Easton said cheerfully as he and Elly entered the breakfast room.

"You are very astute this morning," Benedict retorted while scowling at the paper.

"Ah, yes. Elly did mention something about being up with Jolie during the night," Easton recalled.

"I'm surprised you heard that much," Elly muttered.

"Was she very ill?" Easton enquired.

"She had a nightmare in which something had happened to Margaux, and she was insisting she go to her immediately," Elly explained.

"Perhaps she will have forgotten everything this morning," Benedict said dubiously.

"I doubt it. She was lucid after you left," Elly said.

"How does she mean to travel to Scotland?" Easton asked with a frown.

"She suggested going post with her maid," she replied.

"I do not think I could in good conscience leave Father right now."

"Nor does she expect you to. I told her we could not leave him, but she could not go unless she had a proper chaperone."

"I cannot like the idea. If something has happened, my uncle will send word," Easton reasoned. "I do not think he would approve of me allowing her to go alone."

"We shall find someone. Perhaps Lydia and Nathaniel could go," Elly suggested.

"Unfortunately, he has his hands full with another project at the moment."

"And Andrew and Gwen have the new baby," Elly said, thinking aloud.

"I know of no one else I would trust to accompany her to go so far a distance. She is not unreasonable," he insisted.

Benedict harrumphed.

Easton continued, "She will have to be made to understand."

Benedict coughed.

"Understand what?" Jolie asked from the doorway, donned in a travelling dress of primrose as footmen carried her trunks behind her.

"Are you going somewhere, Jolie?" Easton asked.

"To Scotland. Did Elly not tell you?" she answered, looking a bit exasperated.

"But we have no chaperone for you," Elly explained.

"Then I shall have to make do with my maid. I must go. The feelings continue and have not lessened." She glanced sideways at Benedict, looking mildly embarrassed.

"Jolie, I cannot send you to Scotland with only a maid. There would be no one to go for help should you need it. Some of the roads are extremely remote," Easton said apologetically.

"May I not borrow some of the veterans or grooms as outriders?"

"I would have sent you under their protection had I realised you would need to go. As it is, I have no more to spare that are capable. I'm sorry, Jolie. I do believe your father will send the word if something has happened."

"But he and my mother are on their way back to London. He said as much in his letter to me. I had hoped to intercept them and return with them," she said, growing desperate to plead her case.

Easton and Elly cast glances at each other.

"Perhaps we could persuade Lady Fairmont, but I had hoped to also send a gentleman with you who could actually protect you."

Benedict had been watching this interlude quietly from the table. When he saw Beaujolais' genuine distress and the dilemma the Eastons were faced with, and no further suggestions were forthcoming, he spoke up.

"I will take you."

He was met with three blank stares of astonishment.

"I beg your pardon?" Jolie blinked in confusion.

"I will speak to my mother. She cannot object to helping if you are willing to allow Charlotte to remain here."

"Of course. Charlotte is always welcome," Elly said.

Benedict pushed back his chair and stood. "If you will excuse me, I will make arrangements as quickly as possible. I believe arousing my mother from slumber will be the most difficult part of the arrangement," he said with a smile and left the room.

After Yardley left the room, Jolie was astounded. She had done nothing to warrant such kind treatment from him. In fact, she would have expected him to sit and laugh at her rather than help.

"That was unexpected," Elly remarked.

"You both do Benny an injustice. He is one of the most honourable men I know."

"I know that, but he and Jolie have hardly been on the best of terms. It is quite an effort to escort someone to Scotland," Elly replied to Easton.

Jolie stood and began to pace nervously.

"She is right. I cannot ask it of him. Why must I be a woman? If it were Charles, he would take off and no one would say a word."

"I'm sorry, Jolie. But if you insist on going then I must insist you accept his escort. I have no one else," her cousin replied.

She nodded. "I need to consider. I will be in the garden."

Half an hour later she heard footsteps approaching along the gravel. She had not come to any conclusion other than she must go to her sister. She was making herself sick thinking about being indebted to Yardley, yet not being with Margaux. She still did not feel just the thing, and wished her feelings about her sister would go away and she could simply return to bed.

"Are you ready?"

Jolie looked up to see Yardley dressed for riding.

"I do not know what to say," she said meekly, attesting to her desperation.

"There is little to say but thank you." He held out his hand. "Shall we go? We have a long journey ahead."

She took his hand as he led her to the front drive. A carriage was being loaded with trunks and another with baskets of food.

"How did this happen so quickly?"

"Do not ask. I will merely say I'm not opposed to bribing servants. Also, the Duchess is easily appeased with comfits."

Easton and Elly joined them on the drive while they awaited her Grace.

"Are you sure you feel well enough?" Elly asked.

"Well enough," Jolie agreed half-heartedly.

The grooms were bringing Hector and Dido around and Jolie's eyes grew wide with surprise.

"Do not worry. I will trade off riding them. I do not anticipate a repeat of yesterday. We will leave them at my estate in Birmingham tomorrow."

"Might I ask why Hector is leaving Sussex?" Jolie asked with surprise.

"I purchased him from Easton," he remarked casually over his shoulder as he went to mount.

The Duchess meandered out of the house holding her fluffy white cat and gave her appreciation to the Eastons for looking after Charlotte. However, Jolie thought she detected a measure of relief from her.

She climbed into the carriage after the Duchess and they were on their way before she could think better of it.

Chapter Fourteen

Jolie watched with amusement while the Duchess settled herself and her cat, Daphne, into the opulent blue velvet interior. The inside of the carriage was unlike any she had seen—it had an upholstered bridge between the two seats for the Duchess to recline on. Perhaps it mattered not to her whether she reclined in a carriage or on a drawing room couch, Jolie considered, and she worried less about any imposition she was causing.

The Duchess petted and kissed her cat before she explored the basket of food Cook had prepared to indulge her and the feline. She never once asked why they were making the trip, or what she thought was wrong with Jolie's sister. Yardley must have satisfied her curiosity—if she had any.

"Would you care for one?" she asked, holding out a basket of comfits and biscuits, while taking a bite of another.

"Not at the moment, thank you."

"Please help yourself," she said pleasantly, feeding every other bite of her biscuit to Daphne.

Jolie turned to observe Yardley from the carriage window, once the Duchess had satisfied her palate and was napping. He was magnificent atop Hector, who was behaving well so far today. She did notice he was riding far enough ahead and fast enough to make Hector mind his manners. She chuckled, remembering the disastrous ride in the rain.

When she could no longer see Yardley, she resolved to open the book Elly had lent her to pass the time. Elly had reassured her that it would be worth her while. She was not much given to reading, but there was little else to occupy her. She glanced at the Duchess, who was leaning back into the corner of the coach, her bonnet askew. Jolie smiled to herself and had to stifle a laugh when the lady snorted in her slumber.

She opened to the book's first page and was highly amused by the opening line. A promising start. Daphne jumped over to Jolie's lap to see what was amusing, either that or she was not receiving enough attention from her mistress.

Jolie sneezed as the affectionate kitty rubbed her face all over her, until a hand was occupied in petting her satisfactorily. Daphne settled herself on her lap, making it difficult to see her book.

"Very well, I shall pet you for a few minutes," Jolie conceded.

She set the book aside and began to rub the cat's head and back. Mounds of hair began to come free in her hand. She brushed the hairs off and sent them dancing in the air. She felt her eyes begin to water and a chain of sneezes poured forth.

"What? Huh?" murmured the Duchess, aroused from her slumber.

As Jolie continued to sneeze, the Duchess beat on the roof and ordered the driver to stop. "Stop this carriage! At once!" she demanded.

"I am quite well, I assure you," Jolie protested as the carriage pulled to a stop.

"Out, out," the Duchess shooed.

Jolie climbed from the carriage after the footman had opened the door and put the steps down.

Yardley had turned around when he had noticed the entourage halt its progress and was trotting back towards them.

"Is something amiss?" he asked a confused Jolie.

"I am uncertain," she answered.

He dismounted and looked into the carriage to enquire of his mother.

"Well, why have you stopped not five miles from our departure?"

The Duchess's voice came from inside the carriage. "She is ill! You said it was merely a chill. You know I catch everything if someone who is infirm so much as looks at me! She will have to ride up front with the coachman or in the baggage cart."

Yardley and Jolie stood stunned and speechless. Jolie looked at Dido warily, tied up behind the carriage.

"I shall ride Dido, if you've no objection. My saddle is in the baggage cart?"

Yardley paused and looked at her with an uncharacteristic twinkle in his eye.

"I've no objection, especially since my mother has thrown you from the carriage. However, if there is a repeat performance of yesterday's play, my mother will likely turn back."

"If there is a repeat of yesterday, you will be riding with your mother," she warned.

The horses were well behaved, well enough for Yardley to ride near enough and indulge in conversation for part of the way.

"Do you feel ill? You do not look ill," he remarked as he studied her profile.

"Thank you," she said sardonically. "I feel perfect. I believe I inhaled a bit of Daphne's fluff."

"Perhaps Mother will be convinced by tomorrow. I do not expect you shall wish to ride for the entirety of England."

"I would have done, had it been allowable."

"I suppose we could take my curricle from Yardley. I do not travel well in confined coaches," he continued. "We will not make the time we would on horseback, and we are travelling slower as it is."

"I am perfectly content to ride," she repeated, seemingly to herself.

"I hope you do not object to a night at my estate. It is on the way," he added. "It did not seem the proper thing to make these two cantankerous beasts Easton's responsibility when Wyndham was ill."

"I am certain you are correct," she agreed.

"I will be keeping the foal, so it makes sense to allow Dido to birth at Yardley."

"I would love to see the offspring of these two magnificent animals," she said longingly.

"Perhaps one day you shall," he said quietly.

They cantered on in silence, and Jolie pondered this amicable change in their relationship.

Suddenly, she felt a strong weight upon her chest, which was making it difficult to breathe. She had the overpowering sense that something horrible was happening to Margaux, and that her sister was in grave danger. Tears began to stream down Jolie's face, her throat tightened and she fought back unshed emotion. As she tensed, Dido sped up nervously. She could hear Yardley approaching behind her.

"Jolie," he called after her.

She tried to wipe the tears from her face. She did not wish for him to see her so full of emotion again.

"Jolie!" he called again. His voice shook with concern.

She forced Dido to slow so he could pull abreast, but she continued to look forward.

"Has something happened? Is it your sister?"

She nodded and the tears flowed freely.

Without a word, he grabbed her reins. Pulling the horses to the side of the road, he slowed them to a halt. He gently lifted her chin so she was facing him. Pain seared her neck. She had to stop herself from screaming as she clutched at the burning sensation on her skin. She had to focus on her breathing to retain some sense.

Before she knew what was happening, Yardley had wrapped his arms around her and was comforting her. His scent of sandalwood and the warmth of his arms encompassed her.

"I do not know what to say. I am terribly sorry," he said softly.

She nodded into the comfort of his chest, and suddenly felt the weight lift.

"Is she...?" he left the word unspoken.

"I thought so for certain, but now I am not," she said with a wrinkled brow.

"Forgive me, I have no idea what to say, but I will do whatever I can to help you."

"You must think me a fool," she murmured.

"No. But though I do not pretend to understand, I am sincere in my desire to help," he said earnestly.

"That is something *I* do not pretend to understand."

"Can you not?" he asked, searching her eyes.

For a moment, Jolie thought he was going to kiss her. Their heads dipped closer together and her heart began to pound. But the sound of the carriage approaching pulled them apart and she righted herself on Dido.

"Botheration!" she heard Yardley mutter.

~*~

"This is going to be easier than I thought," a man muttered from behind a tree, as he watched the scene before him unfold. "I will have him eating out of the palm of my hand in less than four-and-twenty hours." He chuckled to himself. "I do not know why women have to make everything more complicated. There is no need to kidnap the chit when a better plan falls right into your lap." He continued to observe Yardley and Lady Beaujolais. "On second thought, she is tempting…"

~*~

The remainder of the day's journey was passed in relative calm and quiet, only stopping for fresh horses and necessities. Neither of them knew quite what to say to the other, but Benedict felt the relationship had changed. He did not wish to take advantage of Jolie's sorrow. She was alone and vulnerable, and his heart ached at seeing her upset. Did she welcome his attentions, or was she too consumed by grief and anguish to notice it was his arms that comforted her?

The latter was more probable, he mused. She would likely be ringing a peal over him by nightfall, and he had found he preferred the spirited Jolie to the one who wept in his arms. He did not like the way his heart wrenched when she was in pain.

The weather was favourable and they covered sixty miles of exceptional road that day, hoping to make Yardley House by the next. The Duchess kept largely to herself in her boudoir on wheels. As the sun waned in the sky, they stopped for the night at an inn near Woking, to where a servant had ridden ahead to bespeak rooms.

Benedict was slightly stiff as he dismounted from his horse, and he tried not to laugh when he saw Jolie attempting to dismount without a grimace. He could not believe that she had ridden the entire journey without complaint. He frequently spent hours in the saddle, whereas she likely took short rides in the city for exercise. He had to admire her resolve, even if it was born from pride and stubbornness.

The footman he had sent ahead was coming towards him with a look of distress.

"What is the matter, Howard?" Benedict enquired.

"They do not have enough rooms, your Grace. There are two, but her Grace would have to share it with the young lady."

Benedict let a sigh of exasperation escape. He was only wanting for food and a bed. However, he knew his mother, and knew she would not be sharing with Lady Beaujolais that night.

"Did you enquire of any nearby inns?"

"I looked myself at the other two nearby. They are full."

"It is too late to go further, and I would not request it of the ladies. Would you ask the innkeeper if I might have a place with the servants?"

The footman's eyes grew wide, but he gave a bow and went back into the inn. Benedict ran his hand through his hair and pondered what to do as he watched his mother stroll into the inn.

"Your Grace," the innkeeper protested as he hurried towards Benedict, just remembering to bow. "You cannot sleep in the stables!"

"It seems there is little choice tonight, Mr Mowbray."

"You shall have my rooms," he insisted. "It will only be a short while for us to prepare them. You may partake of your supper and they shall be ready by the time you have finished."

"I refuse to take your rooms," Benedict argued.

"But, your Grace," the innkeeper pleaded. "It isn't seemly."

~*~

Jolie felt as if she would fall from her horse. She had grown exhausted by mile thirty, however pride had kept her sitting upright in the saddle far beyond the limits of her usual endurance. She had never imagined they could go so far in one day! But she was grateful Yardley seemed to be mindful of expediency.

When they pulled into the Lion's Gate Inn, it was growing dark, and she had to struggle to walk properly as she dismounted. The Duchess alighted from her barouche, looking remarkably spry for someone who had been travelling all day. Her step was cautious, and she gave Jolie a wide berth as she entered the inn lest she might catch her ailment.

Yardley was in discussion with the innkeeper, and it did not look as if the conversation was going well. Frustrated, Jolie walked towards them. Could not Yardley possibly be nice for once? She did not wish to ride any further looking for another place. As she approached, she could hear the exchange.

"But, your Grace, it isn't seemly," the innkeeper said.

Oh, heavens! Was her reputation to be compromised as well? What was the matter?

"I insist," Yardley stated in a ducal voice that brooked no further reply, and expected to be obeyed.

The innkeeper look mortified, but did not argue further, and walked away shaking his head.

"You cannot tell everyone what to do all the time!" Jolie reprimanded.

"Why ever not? I pay them well to be told, and they seem happy to be paid," he objected.

"You should *ask*. Could you not see how upset the man was?"

"And pretend they will not do as I ask anyway? I should have known you would be one of those Wollstonecraft followers," he retorted.

"Because I advocate for decency?" she countered.

"I am not indecent!"

"You do not need to shout."

He shook his head and threw up his hands, then changed the subject.

"Shall we dine? They have laid out a hot meal and I have asked for a bath for you afterwards. If you would prefer to do it in reverse I am certain they would accommodate you."

"No, no. That will be acceptable," she said, mollified by his kindness.

They entered the small parlour, where there was a warm meal waiting for them on the table. The Duchess had decided not to join them. Jolie was perplexed by the woman, and she preferred a distant chaperone to one who was in her way every moment. He held a chair for her before seating himself. Curiosity was eating away at her as she attacked the meat pie rather more voraciously than was ladylike. However, two days' worth of riding had built the appetite.

"Well, are you not going to tell me what you are doing that is unseemly?" she asked, as she followed her bite of pie with a swig of ale.

He looked at her with smug amusement and only shook his head.

"Very well," she replied curtly. "As long as you do not intend to involve me in your unseemliness."

"You are doing quite well on your own."

"Ha!" she muttered. Locking gazes with him, she stuffed another forkful of pie in her mouth.

He returned her stare and with a twinkle in his tawny eyes, took a civilised bite from his own pie.

As soon as the plates were cleared, a maid knocked and entered to show Jolie to her room, where her bath was waiting for her. A groom followed the maid in to direct Yardley.

"Good night, Yardley," she said formally, with a slight curtsy that was painful to execute, though she did not flinch.

"Good night, Lady Beaujolais. I trust you pass a comfortable night."

~*~

With the strange remark repeating itself in her head, Jolie followed the maid up a flight of stairs to a surprisingly well-appointed room for a small inn. It was decorated in hues of blue and gold, with a thick carpet and blue velvet curtains. A small escritoire with a fauteuil sat in the corner, and a gold Ormolu clock ticked on the mantle. A large mahogany four-poster bed contrasted with the walls, which were papered with blue designs.

Jolie's abigail had already set out her soap and cloth for her bath, and she could not wait for the luxury of soaking her aching bones.

"Can I be getting you anything else?" the maid asked.

"I think we have everything we need. You might see if the Duchess is comfortable," Jolie suggested.

"Oh she's tucked up all right and tight. The Duke, however..." the girl said with a frown.

Jolie could tell the girl was concerned. She was not one to normally encourage servants' gossip, but she was consumed with curiosity. Yardley had done nothing but be overly proper since the start of the journey.

"Is something wrong with the Duke?"

"Not wrong 'xactly." The maid shifted her feet nervously as she likely thought better of gossiping about his Grace.

"Then what is it?" Jolie asked impatiently, while at the same time wondering if she really wanted to know.

"He be insisting on sleeping in the stables!" the maid exclaimed. "There weren't no more room, and he would not take Mr Mowbray's room."

"The stables?" Jolie almost stuttered.

"Aye."

"If that is his choice, who are we to question?" Although inside herself, Jolie questioned it very much. She could not imagine sleeping in the stables after a hard day's ride.

"Yes, m'lady." The girl bobbed a curtsy and left the room.

Jolie wandered over to a seat by the window to have her abigail remove her boots from her aching feet. The room overlooked the stableyard, and she shook her head. What was Yardley about? As her maid returned to pour the last bucket of steaming water into the tub, Jolie realised guiltily that Yardley was unlikely to be having the luxury of a bath. Had he given up his room for her? She looked out of the window and barely discerned through the darkness a man splashing his face with water from a trough.

She stopped unlacing her boots and stood.

"Yardley?" she called out to him.

He stepped back into the shadows. "Is your bath cold? Is your mattress lumpy? Are your sheets damp?" he called back in a provoking tone.

"Is my bath cold? You mean *your* bath?"

She turned and ran down the stairs out to the courtyard, where she was astonished to find him stripped of his shirt and scrubbing blissfully with a bar of soap as his valet stood by with a towel. She stopped in her tracks. Thankfully, in the darkness her flushing face should not be obvious, she thought as belatedly she averted her eyes.

"Why are you bathing in public?"

"I would hardly call this public. It is dark, and if eyes were where they are supposed to be, they would not be offended."

"I did not say I was offended," she quipped, her tongue replying before she had a chance to consider.

"That is a relief," he rejoined.

"Would you please go to your room where you belong? I will gladly sleep with my maid."

"Do not be ridiculous."

"Sleeping in the stables is ridiculous!"

"Wasting a warm bath is ridiculous."

"Pray go and enjoy it."

He looked to his valet and taking the towel, dried himself off. "That will be all for now."

The valet nodded and left them alone in the courtyard.

"Yardley, be reasonable. I will not question your gentlemanliness. You have already sacrificed too much on my account. I insist."

"By asking this of me, you question my gentlemanliness."

"Oh, you are exasperating!"

"And I would like to wring your neck," he said, as he walked toward the road behind the inn.

"Where are you going?" she asked with disbelief as she followed him.

"To cool down before I kiss you in front of anyone who might chance to see. Now go and take your bath," he took long strides away, leaving her staring after him.

She turned and began to walk reluctantly back to her room and the bath. She would not be able to enjoy it as much knowing he had bathed in the trough—not to mention the image of him stripped to the waist that she would not be able to forget.

"And what would be so horrid about kissing me?" she asked aloud to herself, wondering why he had said it as if it would be distasteful to do so. On the thought, she spun around and hurried back to where she had left him.

He was standing in the moonlight looking upwards, and he turned at her approach with eyebrows raised.

Rational thinking played no part in her reaction. She walked right over to Yardley, stood toe to toe with him—and his still-bared torso—reached up to kiss him. It certainly was not what she expected, although her thoughts were so muddled, she could not be sure what she expected. Somehow, her arms wrapped themselves around his neck and his hands were holding her face. It was not a gentle kiss as their lips locked furiously. It contained pent-up attraction and emotion and went on for some time before Jolie regained her senses. She was acutely aware of his masculinity and her own vulnerability. He smelt fresh and clean with soap, and his skin...what was she doing?

She pulled away abruptly, leaving a stunned Yardley staring at her.

"Oh!" Her hands flew to her face.

"Why did you stop? I was not finished," he asked with dismay.

His answer was a slap in the face.

"Would you mind telling me what that was for?" he asked.

"I did not want to kiss you!" she exclaimed.

"It certainly felt as though you did," he retorted, rubbing his cheek where she had slapped him.

She threw up her hands with a squeak of annoyance and stormed off. He trailed after her while pulling his shirt back over his head.

"Do not follow me! What if someone sees you like that?" she whispered loudly.

He stopped.

"This is not finished, Beaujolais," he said quietly.

"Oh, yes, sir, it is. Good night." She turned and hastened back into the inn and up the stairs, furious with herself.

As she rounded the top of the stairs to the hallway, she heard a loud thud and a groan. She looked up to find the Duchess standing there, in her nightdress and cap, holding a poker over a man, who was face down on the floor.

"What happened?" Jolie asked, rushing to her side.

"I was looking out to find a maid. They did not answer the bell, and poor Daphne needed her bedtime milk," she explained as the man on the floor groaned again. "I saw this man trying to sneak into Benedict's room, so I grabbed the poker and hit him."

"Oh, dear!" Jolie exclaimed. "Should we call for help?"

"I have done. My maid arrived soon afterwards, and she is retrieving the innkeeper."

At length, the innkeeper and Yardley came rushing to the farcical scene to find the Duchess with her bed cap askew, holding a poker over a man, while the cat licked his face.

Yardley walked over to the man and rolled him over.

"Dannon?" he said with surprise as the man groaned.

"Dannon?" the rest of the group exclaimed.

Holding his head, the man on the floor looked owlishly up at the innkeeper. "I mistook the room number."

"Ye also mistook the inn," the innkeeper said doubtfully. "Ye were told we're full."

Yardley pulled Dannon to his feet. "We shall continue this conversation elsewhere."

Jolie watched as he hauled Dannon away, with the innkeeper following behind. Had it not been Lord Dannon who had been with Madame Clement in Brighton? What a strange coincidence to see him here also. She helped the Duchess, who seemed nonplussed by the event, back into her room. The maid fussed over her and brought her a tisane.

"Thank you, Gussie. That will be all," the Duchess said.

Jolie also started to leave, but her Grace spoke. "You might wish to be more cautious on a moonlit night."

Jolie felt warmth creeping up her neck. "I beg your pardon?" Surely she could not be referring to...

"Daphne was meowing at the window. I happened to look out to see what the fuss was about."

"I...I..." Jolie could not believe she was having this conversation. She did not know how to respond.

"I rather thought it was a clever move on your part," the Duchess said, sipping her tisane, as Jolie's jaw nearly hit the floor. "I will be delighted if he finally overcomes his obsession with Lillian. Ten years of servitude is quite long enough. Good night."

"Good night, your Grace." Jolie was thankful to escape any more of the Duchess' thoughts, for she had enough of her own to torment her.

Chapter Fifteen

Benedict stood in the courtyard for some time, longing to run in after Lady Beaujolais. He was growing more concerned about the depth of Lillian and Dannon's desperation. He had paid handsomely to have Dannon escorted back to London, with several men to guard him, and have him delivered to Lord Fairmont. There was little he could do with Dannon at this point, but separating him geographically was a start. He did not want to be involved in whatever Dannon's latest nefarious scheme was, but he had little doubt Lillian was involved. His greater concern was for Lady Beaujolais. What if she had been in the room? Was Dannon looking for her, or for himself? This woman had turned upside down both his thoughts and feelings, and he felt an overwhelming urge to protect her. He shook his head and went to the stables.

With not enough room at the inn, Benedict empathised with Joseph and Mary as he turned over and a piece of straw jabbed him in the back where his coat did not reach. At least he was not accompanying an expectant wife, but sleeping in the stables after a hard ride was as close as he had ever come to torture. He would not complain, however, for he had heard tell of stories of soldiers enduring far worse conditions for months, even years, in extreme temperatures, with few provisions, and no horses to walk for them. He could at least take pride in the fact that his own grooms all slept on cots at Yardley.

Benedict was awake before the cock crowed, though he felt as if he had scarcely slept. Besides the discomfort, he could not take his mind from Lady Beaujolais. How was he to endure several more weeks of her daily presence? He was anxious to show her Yardley, but nervous at the same time.

He walked into the inn, musing. He was intoxicated by her nearness, yet his anxiety over her rejection and his simultaneous fear of being betrayed again weighed heavily on his thoughts. He could not seem to erase his bitter memories of Lillian, and her reappearance had served only to deepen the wound. The more time he spent with Lady Beaujolais, the less he reasoned she was anything like Lillian. Had not the blinkers been removed a decade prior? Would he not recognise a traitoress staring him in the face? He wanted to believe it of himself, but he knew he was not in his right mind when near her.

He waited in the parlour for the ladies as he substituted poor coffee for sleep. He wished to make Yardley before sunset, in the hope that Jolie would be able to see its splendour, even though it would mean another long day's ride. She was the daughter of a marquess, and was unlikely to be swayed by the grandeur of a ducal seat, but he was partial to the home that had become his salvation in his darkest days, along with his horses. He wanted her to love it as he loved it.

"Good morning, Benedict," his mother greeted him jovially as she entered the parlour.

He stood and embraced her. "I see you are no worse for yesterday's events."

"Why would I be?" she asked as she sat in a chair. "Are we to leave soon? I thought we were making haste. Or is Lady Beaujolais too ill to continue?"

"I imagine she will be down directly. She is not ill, Mother. She did not sneeze once the entirety of the ride."

The Duchess looked somewhat chagrined. "She certainly seemed ill in the barouche."

144

"I cannot believe you chose your cat's comfort over the daughter of a marquess."

"I thought she was ill," she said defensively.

"You should consign the cat to the luggage cart and allow Lady Beaujolais a place in the carriage. She could scarcely walk by the time we arrived last night."

"I suppose she may, if she must. But I did not insist upon her riding the entire way."

He shook his head in dismay. "Have you broken your fast?"

"I have. The birds woke me before the sun was up. I always find inns tiresomely noisy."

"We shall have the reprieve of Yardley tonight if the roads hold up."

"Do you mean to marry this one, then? I assume that is why we are gallivanting about the kingdom for her?"

"She needs our help. Easton could not help, and I could."

"As long as I have a grandchild soon," the Duchess remarked casually as she heaped jam onto her second breakfast of toast. "I hope you do not lose your head this time."

"My head is firmly affixed, Mother," he said, trying not to show his annoyance.

"Shall I send my maid up to see about Lady Beaujolais?"

"There is no need. I am here. I apologise if I have kept you waiting," Lady Beaujolais said as she entered the room, looking smart in her violet-coloured riding habit with a jaunty beaver hat to match.

"Not at all," Benedict said as he rose. "Would you care to break your fast?"

"I have already done so, thank you," she replied.

"How are you feeling this morning?" he asked with a wry smile.

145

"I have no complaints. I imagine I slept a good deal more comfortably than you did," she said, with a raised eyebrow.

He cleared his throat, not wishing to explain the circumstances to his mother, who was nibbling on another slice of toast.

"And how does your sister fare?" he asked, ignoring her remarks.

She gazed upon him with her startlingly violet-blue eyes, looking surprised at his question.

"I have not felt the sensation again," she said in a voice just above a whisper.

"I am glad to hear it. Perhaps whatever happened has passed."

"I wish I knew. I cannot tell," she said. Her lip trembled as she looked away..

He had to restrain himself from comforting her, so he gave her a moment to control her emotion.

"If you are ready, we best be away. It is another long day to my estate, though I trust the night's repose will be worth it."

"Indeed. I am ready."

"Mother?" he enquired.

"Yes, yes. I am ready. Lady Beaujolais, I will put Daphne in the luggage cart if you would like to sit with me," she said graciously.

"That is very kind, your Grace, but I think I would like to ride as long as the day continues to be so lovely," she replied.

"Do let me know if you tire of it. I could never abide more than an hour or so in the saddle myself," the Duchess said before rising from the table and bustling off to her carriage.

"She means well," Benedict told Beaujolais as they followed and walked out to the horses.

"I am not offended. I do not mind riding," she assured him.

"Shall I assist you?" He indicated the saddle.

"Yes, thank you."

He inhaled the sweet scent of her—a mixture of honey and vanilla—as he cupped his hands to boost her up into the saddle. She seemed so small and fragile, yet she exuded strength from the inside. He did not wish to let her go.

~*~

The manor was nestled amongst a copse of trees, atop a hill presiding over an expansive vale. Jolie could see hints of the house's golden grandeur as they made their way up the winding path. The sun was reflecting deep pink and orange hues on the horizon in the late evening sky, and the fresh scents of summer—blossoms and grasses—wafted in the breeze.

Her pulse quickened with excitement to see the park as they grew near. She felt as if she were glimpsing into a secret chamber—something forbidden that few were allowed to see. They passed through a quaint village, adorned with thatched roofs and gardens of wild flowers, before turning through the gates to the park. Yardley stopped and inhaled a deep breath as he surveyed his land, and she could see the tension leave his face and be replaced with pride. She could not help but smile as she witnessed a master and his domain.

"There is something I would like to show you, if you are not too tired. We must set off early tomorrow, and I prefer this view at sunset."

"I would love to see it," she said in earnest.

"You are most welcome to see anything you wish."

He turned his horse down a pathway she would not have noticed otherwise. They followed it through a canopy of pine trees for some distance, until it opened upon a breathtaking waterfall which flowed down into the valley below. They dismounted and allowed the horses graze.

"We call this place the Hidden Falls. I have yet to find anywhere else to view them," he said fondly.

They stood for a moment, at one with Nature, and she felt at peace— even with Yardley. He was near enough that she could feel the heat from him and smell the evidence of a day's ride.

"*C'est beau*," she said quietly, and she felt him stiffen. She turned to look at him, and his face was stern. Had she said something wrong?

"We had best return before dark," he said tersely, placed her back on her horse, then mounted his own.

They rode in silence to the house, and Jolie could not discern what she had done to offend him. Her first view of the house in its entirety was as the sun was setting, shining magnificent rays onto its golden stone. The house was a masterpiece of Baroque design, enhanced by arched windows that reflected the sun's last effort of the day. It was a shame she would have so little time here; she longed to explore and know every inch of the house and park.

She would have given almost anything for a few moments to escape to the gardens, to have time for the simplicity of feeding the birds. She needed to be free of Yardley's overwhelming presence for a while, in order to think properly. But there was little time for any such luxury, and she must endure the struggle to focus on her sister and reach her. She continued to have vague sensations about Margaux, but none as strong as the ones where she had been certain of her sister's pain. The uncertainty was agonising.

He had regained his composure by the time he helped her from the saddle, and appeared to be at ease when they entered the house.

The doors were opened to them by a butler scarcely older than her, who wore a patch over one eye. Jolie wondered if he had been in one of the recent wars. It was strange to have such a young man in the role, but she was happy to see evidence of a pleasant household as she received a friendly smile from him. Her eyes were instantly drawn upwards to three-storeyed windows and then around the hall to the intricate white plasterwork on the walls and ceilings. An ornate chandelier hung from the centre of the ceiling, and more Baroque-style carvings adorned a banister that circled its way around the hall.

"Welcome to Yardley Park, Lady Beaujolais," the Duke remarked. "This is Childers, our butler."

"We are delighted to welcome you, Lady Beaujolais," the young man said eloquently. "Will you be dining formally tonight, your Grace? Marsden is prepared, if that is your wish."

Yardley looked to Jolie. "Do you prefer to take a tray in your room, or would you prefer to dine with my mother and me?"

"I have never been one for dining in seclusion," she remarked.

"Then shall we say an hour? There should be a bath awaiting you."

She could overlook many of his faults for his consideration of her bathing. "Yes, thank you. I can manage in an hour."

"The housekeeper will show you to your room. Your maid should be prepared for you, but do not hesitate to ring if you need anything. I hope you will find your apartments pleasing."

"I am certain they shall exceed my expectations. It is not a stable, after all," she bantered, but his reaction was distant and he only nodded before walking away.

The bath beckoned to her, but she could not resist catching a glimpse of the view from the room before complete darkness fell. The view over the valley was mesmerising, with sheep dotting the hillside and fields of wheat and barley alternating with forested woodlands. She spied the edge of a garden to the side of the house, which was bursting with the bright colours of rhododendrons and lilies, and she hoped to find a moment to stroll through it before leaving. She realised she felt tranquil. It was the first time she could recall feeling this way since she had parted from her family. It was strange to think she was now a guest in Yardley's house after everything that had passed between them, yet she still felt a sense of belonging.

She turned to her bath, and took a closer look at the apartment as she sank into the luxuriously warm water. It was a decidedly feminine room, done in pale greens, and embellished with lavenders and violets. A landscape hung on the wall opposite. It appeared to be in the style of Gainsborough, with the subject a horse, of course. There was a staircase in one corner of the room, and Jolie was curious to explore its destination. She reluctantly rose from the bath and readied for dinner, thinking she had been hasty in her refusal of a tray in this peaceful sanctuary.

Her feet were compelled to explore the staircase, and she decided it was logical that the circular steps led to somewhere on the floor below, and where the dining room was situated. As she descended, she could hear the faint sounds of a pianoforte and she was drawn, without consciousness, toward the sound.

~*~

When Benedict saw Beaujolais walking through his house, his home, she made each room appear brighter, more vibrant than ever before. He would no longer see this room without her as its centrepiece, he thought, as he saw her coming down the steps from the mistress's apartments above to this sanctuary, shared between his room and hers. Lillian had never bothered to grace it with her presence.

He had taken a moment of solace to pour out his emotion through Beethoven's *Moonlight Sonata*, and he froze when he saw her. He never played for anyone save himself. It was a private refuge for him.

"Do not stop," she said softly as she approached. His eyes locked with hers.

His hands betrayed him, continuing with the song as she sat down beside him, barely fitting on the seat. He was instantly intoxicated by her warmth, her scent, by her. One of her hands joined his on the piano keys, and they began to play the song together. She could not have seduced him more completely had she walked into the room unclothed. He could not understand why he was baring his soul to this woman, but he could only watch it happen.

The song finished, and they sat in silence for some minutes, his pulse racing and his breathing shallow. He could not speak the words he longed to say. He was being consumed by her, yet he could not bear the thought of her rejection. He chose to savour this perfect moment.

But as he sat breathing in rhythm with her, he felt an overwhelming need to touch more than the ivory on the pianoforte. Leaning over her, he brought her face up towards him.

"Jolie," he uttered, willing her to understand his need for her, as he drew her towards him, gently and tentatively. At first his lips brushed hers with the slightest touch of their noses. But he needed this. He needed to kiss her, to know her. Teasing her lips gently, he slowly pressed his lips to hers in a sensual rhythm. His hands moved up her back and into her hair, while her arms found their way around his neck. While the keys had not stirred in minutes, music was still moving through their passionate embrace. Panting, their breathing mingled, then he pulled back and whispered to her, "Jolie, we should stop."

Both stood, attempting to comprehend what had happened. They realised they had lost track of time and of their senses. They hurriedly began to right themselves as they recalled they were expected at the dinner table.

The Duchess looked knowingly at the two of them, as they were late to dinner. Her fork was perched over her plate.

"I was about to begin without you," she remarked.

"Forgive us. We were lost in Beethoven."

She scoffed without looking up, and pierced her stuffed pigeon.

Benedict could have let dinner rot for all the appetite he still had. He was not hungry for food. It had been a long day in the saddle, and his mother carried the conversation while he and Beaujolais remained largely silent. His mind was consumed with Beaujolais, and how to continue later the enchanting interlude they had experienced only moments before. He wondered if she had been as affected as he.

~*~

Jolie awoke to the sounds of summer as dawn was beginning to break. She hurried to dress in order to explore before Yardley and his mother awakened. The evening before, she had seen a bridge across the lake. As she walked in that direction, it was to the song of the birds and the trickle of the fountain in the formal gardens near the house. She kept going past the well-manicured hedges surrounded by statues, towards the unruly wild gardens beyond.

She inhaled deeply of the fresh summer foliage. This was the allure of the country…the intoxicating scent of hydrangeas; the vibrant deep pink hues of rhododendrons, the newly-born birds chirping, the wet dew on her boots…she could almost forget why she was here. She plucked some daisies and held them to her nose as she spun about with happiness. She hurried onto the bridge as the sun crept over the house, greeting her with rays upon her face.

As she crossed the bridge, she could see another building across the parkland framed by trees. Oh, to not be rushed and to lose herself here for a while. Her family had lived in the country in France before they were forced to leave by Napoleon's tyranny, and she had spent most of her time in London since. Had she truly been so foolish as to refuse this? No. It had not been unwise, she reminded herself. Accepting Yardley's offer as it had been made would have been foolish. But she was so very tempted to run to him and beg him to reconsider. Would he?

She stepped onto the path from the bridge leading towards what appeared to be a mausoleum, or burial ground, for the Yardley dynasty. It would be hard to imagine a more peaceful resting place. The lake was surrounded by lush green vegetation and she savoured one more moment before turning to walk the path to the house, as the sun peeped through the canopy of trees.

She noticed a messenger riding up the drive to the house. It could not yet be six of the clock. Could something be wrong? Had her father traced her to here with a message? She lifted her skirts and with anxiety giving wings to her feet, set off running.

"What has happened?" she asked breathlessly as she entered the house. Yardley looked up distractedly from the missive and held it out to her.

Your Grace,

I am writing from Paris. Lord Fairmont, Lord Easton and I thought it best if I attempted to discover why Madame Clement and Lord Dannon suddenly reappeared in England after all these years, and why Dannon would take such a risk to return. My investigations thus far indicate they left here in a hurry. Monsieur Clement died recently under suspicious circumstances, and it appears Lord Dannon was not welcomed in polite circles this side of the Channel, either. I will continue searching for the connection between the Clements and Dannon. It grows suspicious.

Your servant,
Hughes

Chapter Sixteen

It felt as though it had taken an age to finally reach Breconrae, and when they arrived at the estate, they passed by the Dower House, which had been devastated by fire. Jolie sucked in her breath, fearing her sensations of Margaux's pain had been right all along. Her eyes filled with tears as they continued on the path to the main house.

As they turned the corner, half of the main house was in ruins and she cried out in fear.

"No!"

Yardley took her hand and held it as they pulled to the front of the house. It did comfort her, and she found she did not wish to release it.

"Let me see if I can find someone to ask before we assume the worst," he said, as he jumped down from the carriage.

Jolie tried to remain hopeful, but the grounds appeared deserted. She fretted through the worst of emotions—fearing her sister dead—as Yardley was gone longer than she had expected. He returned with a groom.

"This is Callum, and he says the family has been staying at the adjoining Craig Castle since the fire. The Solstice Ball is taking place this evening."

"And Lady Margaux is unharmed?" she asked anxiously.

The groom averted his eyes. "No, m'lady. She was hurt, but she is recovering."

"Thank God," Jolie sighed with relief, as she covered her face with her hands.

Yardley jumped back in beside her.

The groom proceeded to give directions, and they rode the short distance in silence. Their arrival was scarcely noticed as servants bustled about performing last-minute preparations for the Ball. The butler immediately sent for Lord Ashbury. By the look on his face, it appeared he had perceived Jolie's likeness to Margaux.

They were shown to a comfortable study, and Jolie was examining the portrait of the incumbent family when her father entered the room.

"Jolie," he exclaimed as he crossed the room with his arms open wide. "Whatever are you doing here?"

She embraced her father with an enormous sense of relief. "I felt something happen to Margaux. I could not stay away."

"Indeed it did." He held her back at arms' length. "Let us take a seat."

Lord Ashbury started when he noticed Yardley across the room.

"Papa, this is the Duke of Yardley."

Her father held out his hand to greet him. "Welcome. I do believe I have seen you before. Thank you for bringing Jolie to us."

"My pleasure. Easton did not feel he could leave Wyndham right now. My mother also accompanied us, and has been shown to a room," he explained.

Ashbury held out his arm to indicate for Yardley to sit.

"You must already know there was a fire, if you stopped at Breconrae."

Jolie nodded.

"Margaux was trapped in the fire, but Lord Craig was able to save her."

Jolie sucked in her breath.

"He sent for us and we turned around near the border. Margaux has some injuries, but she has recovered remarkably since we first arrived. I am certain she will tell you the story herself."

"I am very happy to hear she is recovering. I have not felt the sense of pain so strongly as we became closer to here."

"Her voice is diminished and she has some scars, so prepare yourself. Your mother did not anticipate the change and she swooned when she saw her."

"*Maman* swooned?" Jolie asked in disbelief.

He nodded. "You had best ready yourself for the Ball, and then you should go to Margaux before dinner."

"Very well. I was not expecting a ball. I hope we can manage so quickly," she said as she stood.

"Oh, there is one more thing," her father said holding his finger in the air. "Margaux has married Lord Craig."

"I beg your pardon?" she asked in disbelief.

"Indeed. Is it not remarkable?" He chuckled, and turned to lead them up the staircase.

~*~

Jolie's mind was in a whirl as she hastened to prepare for the ball. *Margaux was married.*

What could have happened to bring it about? Margaux had been fiercely opposed to the institution when she had left London. That was why she was in Scotland! There had better be a very good explanation, or she would drag her sister back to England.

Her maid put the finishing touches to her toilette, and Jolie walked to Lady Craig's apartments.

The door to the room opened, and Margaux and her apparent husband stepped out. Jolie could not take her eyes from her sister as she searched for her injuries.

"Jolie?" Margaux said with obvious shock. "Is it really you?"

"So it is true, then?" Jolie said none too happily as she looked from Margaux to her husband, to whom Margaux was linked arm in arm. "How could you?"

"Welcome to our home, Lady Beaujolais. I trust your journey was uneventful?" Lord Craig bowed to her as if she had not just insulted him and his wife.

She looked at him, incredulous.

"You remember Dr Craig, do you not?" Margaux asked calmly.

"I...I..." The moment of recognition crossed Jolie's face as she finally looked to the man. "But..."

"I have only recently come into the title on the death of my brother," Lord Craig explained.

"Forgive me, Lord Craig. One would think someone might have mentioned that minor detail. You have not quite married a stranger then, have you? I was prepared to take drastic measures."

"I entered into this marriage of my own volition, Jolie," Margaux said quietly.

"If you will pardon me, ladies, I think I would rather not be present for this conversation." Lord Craig smiled. "Shall I have trays sent up so you may continue this in private? I am certain everyone will understand, as long as you are down in time for the receiving line."

"Thank you, my lord. I believe that to be an excellent idea," Jolie answered, and dragged her sister back into her room.

"Why, yes, Jolie, I will neglect my guests and join you in here. Thank you for consulting me," Margaux said sarcastically.

"Oh, Marg!" She gathered her sister up in a hug. Her sister tensed.

"What is the matter? Oh! Is it the burns? Do they still pain you? You look so fine, I had forgotten."

"I am healing. The burns are still sensitive to the touch, but are thankfully hidden beneath the gown and gloves."

"Are they very bad?"

"They could have been much worse. The housekeeper died," Margaux said quietly.

"I knew, you know. I could sense something was wrong that night. It was horrible to feel you were in danger, and I did not know how. It took me ages to arrange a chaperone and to travel here. Then I am told you are married! You of all, married." She held her hands wide to emphasise the enormity of the event.

"Yes."

"That is all you can say? You, who shunned a dozen eligible suitors in London; you, who objected to marriages of convenience; you, who declared you would only marry for love. I understand a little after realising you were acquainted, but can you truly tell me you formed a *tendre* for him before you married? You have never been a hypocrite."

Margaux was visibly angry. She turned away and looked out the window.

"Why are you here, Jolie? If you have come to rant at me about my marriage, then save your breath. It is done. Why should it bother you? You yourself are perfectly willing to marry for convenience. Or can you tell me you are in love with Yardley?"

"I never pretended to want a love-match."

Margaux sighed. "Very well. Continue."

Jolie's shoulders sagged. "It is not as much fun if you are given permission to scold. I only want to see you happy."

"I know." Margaux walked over to her sister and took her hand.

"We all believed you would come to your senses within a fortnight," Jolie said resignedly.

"I know."

"I never could have imagined you would be married already."

"I did not, either."

"Did something happen to make it necessary?"

"No!" Margaux dropped her sister's hand and pushed at her in a sisterly way. "Not in that way."

"Well, what are we supposed to think?"

"I suppose I came to my senses. It happened so fast. I became an instant pariah, Jolie."

"A pariah? You had a chaperone."

"Aunt Ida?" Margaux asked mockingly.

"That bad? She always was a bit flighty, but a dear."

"She is still a dear, but she is not always here, even when she is."

"Ah. I see. So the prudish little village took a dislike to an independent woman and shunned you. And you were too proud to come back to London with your tail between your legs, and Dr Craig came to your rescue. I suppose you should be so fortunate he was not a pickled old man, stuffed into creaking stays with rotten teeth."

"I believe I would have come to London with my tail between my legs, as you say, before that." Margaux laughed.

"He is extraordinarily handsome, Marg." Jolie's knowing eyes mocked.

"He is," she agreed jovially.

"Are you in love with him now?"

Her sister's eyes pierced through her. She did not have to answer. She lowered her eyes.

160

"When did you arrive? And who came as your chaperone?" Margaux changed the subject.

"I believe it has been a couple of hours now. We were unaware there was to be a ball today until we arrived. I had envisioned you still in the sick room. But I am relieved to know you are not."

"Only you could come straight from the carriage looking ready for a ball. It is to be the tenants' Solstice Ball, however."

"I will try not to embarrass you with my London ways."

Margaux made a face.

"Yardley might."

"You brought Yardley with you?" Margaux could not believe it. "Are you betrothed?"

"No, we are not. And he insisted. As did his mother. I had no one else to accompany me, and I had to come."

Her sister held out her hand, and Jolie took it.

"Dear me. I hope you will explain later." Margaux laughed. "The villagers will be too terrified to step into the house if they know the Duke and Duchess are present."

"They will not know until it is too late. They do know how to behave," she chided.

"Do they? Around those they consider well beneath them?"

"That is unfair, Marg."

"Perhaps. He only disapproves of Society, then."

"It is easy to become jaded when everyone toad-eats you all the time."

"Very well. I will give him another chance. He approves of you, so he cannot be all bad. If he makes you happy, I will try to be happy for you."

"I am not sure." She would tell her sister the whole story later. It was better to let her enjoy the ball. If she knew, she would not be civil to

Yardley. Margaux had never been one to hide her feelings. "There is certainly more to him than I had given him credit for."

"I will be open-minded, then."

Her sister smiled, and Jolie could see the effects of the fire as her skin puckered beneath the rice powder. She reached up and gently stroked the skin. Margaux winced.

"I only want your happiness." Her sister nodded.

"And I yours."

Chapter Seventeen

As they joined the dinner guests in the ballroom, Jolie introduced Yardley to Margaux, and he was amiable and polite. She had to look and make certain it was truly him speaking. She could see Margaux's face held some surprise, before Lord Craig led her away to greet the Duchess.

"It appears your sister is not a spinster any longer," Yardley remarked as they watched Margaux walk away on the arm of her new husband.

"It is most kind of you to point out what would be obvious to our blind pug."

"Is your dog truly blind?" he asked with surprise.

"She is. I would not dare jest of an affliction," Jolie said with mild affront.

"Unless it was mine," he clarified.

"Unless it was yours," she agreed.

"What do you mean to do now?" he asked.

"Enjoy the ball. Are you not to secure any dances?" she asked coyly.

He glanced around the room and said, *"There are none handsome enough to tempt me."*

Thinking his opinion rather rude, but taking no personal offence, she wrinkled her brow in thought. "I have heard that somewhere before, but I cannot place it."

"Then I shall not spoil it for you," he said playfully.

"I should have known you would not put me out of my misery."

"Speaking of misery, Lord Craig has warned me to be on the look-out for the people who set the fire at Breconrae. It is believed they may reappear tonight."

"The fire was intentional?"

"They believe so. There were fires at the Dower House and the main house, if you recall. It would be an uncanny coincidence for both to catch alight within minutes of the other."

"Yes, I suppose so. What a terrible ordeal. And Lord Craig believes the people continue to be a threat? Poor Margaux. I wonder they did not cancel the ball."

"I imagine cancelling the ball would have made the situation worse. Settling this tonight will be best for all concerned."

Jolie saw his gaze wander across the ballroom. Following its direction, she saw her mother and his, seated on a sofa, chatting comfortably.

"What do you think they can be talking about?" she asked.

"Grandchildren."

"Grandchildren? But they haven't any," she said in confusion.

"Precisely."

Yardley led her out for the opening dance as requested by Lord Craig since Margaux could not dance. She also danced with her father and Seamus, then sat out the next dance with an injured veteran before supper. Lord Craig gave an enchanting speech about Margaux, and Jolie knew at once that he was as much in love with her sister as she was with him. She felt a small pang of envy, but an overwhelming sense of relief for Margaux's happiness. As she watched Lord Craig lead Margaux into a slow waltz, Yardley was suddenly at her side and accompanying her to the floor as a few other couples joined in.

"I do believe your sister might have managed a love match," he said in an indifferent tone.

"Yes, I would not have believed it, had I not been a witness."

"Rarely does one find a two-sided love match."

"I know," she said softly. "You do not hold a high opinion of marriage."

"*My good opinion once lost is lost forever.*"

Was he also referring to her refusal? Her heart sank with the truth of his words. She had given her opportunity away and had no right to hope. He did say he had made his choice of bride already.

She looked up to see a twinkle in his eye, and her insides began to flutter. He spun her about and drew her closer, likely scandalising the local tenants.

"I suppose that is why you prefer an arrangement," she remarked. She felt him tense, but he replied.

"It is." He did not elaborate.

He led her through the dance with more spins, leaving her near breathless for a time, lost in the beauty of the music and movement. She loved to waltz, and it was effortless to partner him. It was a surreal experience with Yardley, whose masculinity was softened by the elegance of a gentleman.

"What do you mean to do after tonight?" he asked, disturbing her dreamlike state.

"I do not know. Perhaps look about Scotland for unmarried Dukes," she replied impertinently.

"An acknowledged hit."

The crowd started to part as a woman and small child came forward to Margaux and Lord Craig.

"What is happening?" Jolie asked.

"It must be the people Craig was concerned about. Stay back," Yardley warned as he headed toward Lord and Lady Craig.

"I will not!" Jolie marched directly behind him.

As they approached, she could see the dishevelled woman holding the little girl threateningly in her arms. Jolie stepped next to Margaux as Yardley crept behind the woman.

"You double before my eyes, God save our souls! Seize them!" the woman shouted to the crowd hysterically.

Lord Craig began to direct Margaux and the crazed woman out to the terrace. Where Jolie prayed, he could coerce her into reason away from the audience.

~*~

As they watched them move out to the balcony, Benedict held on to Jolie.

She attempted to loosen her arms and looked up at him. "What are you doing?" she demanded.

"I am holding you back," he replied to her indignant question.

"She is my sister!" she protested.

"And she is being taken care of by your father and her husband. The woman is clearly out of her senses. She might mistake you," he said sternly, as he kept her close.

Jolie looked up into his eyes. He felt like his soul was pouring forth, but he could not tell her how he felt.

"I need to be with Margaux," she pleaded.

"When she is out of harm's way."

"You are insufferable!" she muttered under her breath.

"So you constantly remind me."

They heard a scream from outside on the terrace. Jolie broke forth when Yardley was distracted by the scream, and she ran to her sister.

When they had pushed through the crowd, they saw Margaux being carried away by her father, and Lord Craig rushing down the steps from the terrace.

"Is Margaux harmed?" she asked her mother.

"No, thankfully. Just frightened. Her husband would not be hastening to help that woman if Margaux needed him," Lady Ashbury said, as she hurried after Margaux.

Benedict gently put his arm around Jolie, and led her to a seat. He looked about for a footman, but the scene was just shy of chaos.

The crowd was murmuring with unabashed curiosity, though some of the guests were dispersing. He went himself and found a drink for her. He handed her the glass and she looked up with obvious pique.

"Thank you, sir," she said with cold formality.

"Lady Beau—"

She held up her hand.

"Jolie," he corrected.

"I beg yer pardon, yer Grace, but a message has come for ye." The butler held out a silver tray with a sealed note.

Benedict raised his eyebrows and took the message from the salver.

Your Grace,

My ship was hit by a storm, and we were redirected to Jersey until it passed. Rotten luck, you say? As it happens, Lord Dannon has an estate on the isle, and is rumoured to be running a bordello there that caters to eccentric tastes. This is unverified, though there is oft something to the word of the locals over a pint of ale. One merely has to sift through the embellishments. He was said to be seen in company of a beautiful woman fitting the description of Madame Clement, which is no surprise. I'm returning to London to join forces with Lord Fairmont.

Your obedient servant,

Hughes

Yardley,

My hopes are this letter finds the Ashburys and yourself in good health. I have directed Hughes' letter to you. After reading it, we began to have Lillian followed. She spends a great deal of time at the modiste, *which is not so fantastical...*

We did not hold Dannon, lest we anger Prinny before we have enough information. I have confirmed Prinny received a handsome donation from Dannon. Lydia has threatened to speak with him herself about her uncle's depravity, but I would prefer to keep her out of this. Thus far, Dannon spends a great deal of time frequenting brothels, which surprises no one.

The other news from London is several young girls have gone missing. I have no evidence to form a connection, however my conscience is nagging me to find one. When Hughes arrives, I plan to pursue this. Your help would be most welcome if it is convenient.

Yours etc,

Fairmont

Benedict wanted to scream. While the Ashbury and Craig were dealing with a problem, he had some of his own. He finally felt as if he had a chance with Beaujolais. Even if the chance was miniscule, he had seen a look in her eye tonight that gave him courage. But Lillian was succeeding yet again at interfering in his happiness.

He sighed loudly.

Lady Beaujolais said nothing, but was looking at him expectantly.

"I am required in London," he stated, not wishing to burden her with the letters while she was worried about her sister.

"I hope nothing is amiss," she said with a look of concern.

"Lord Fairmont sends word that he fears Lillian and Dannon may be up to something evil, beyond their normal depravity," he explained as broadly as he could.

"Why is it your affair? She is no longer your wife," Beaujolais asked curtly.

"I wish it were that simple." He wanted to explain, but he needed to have that part of his life closed before he could begin again. Lillian would always come between him and any future he tried to make. It was not enough for her to have almost destroyed him once.

"It is of no consequence. It is not my place to dictate your whims," she said hurriedly as she stood. "I wish to go and see my sister. Good night."

"Of course. Good night." He executed a quick bow. "I'm sorry to have disappointed you," he said to himself as he watched her walk away, thinking Lillian would be wise to leave the country before he found her.

Chapter Eighteen

Jolie walked to the breakfast room in furious debate about what to say to Yardley. She had slept poorly for worrying about it. She longed to confess her admiration for him and her change of heart, but she was too uncertain whether her regard was returned or not. She thought he held her in some esteem, otherwise he would not have escorted her to Scotland. There were many moments when she sensed he cared, but then he appeared indifferent. Regardless of these contradictions, his attentions to his former wife were concerning. Why ever would he be hurrying back to London to help her if his heart was truly disengaged, as he had indicated? Jolie's own heart was heavy—it felt as if he was choosing between them, which logic told her was ridiculous.

They had shared much in a very little time, including passionate kisses, though she knew men felt differently about such things. At least, according to her brother, they did.

She was forced to sit through a jovial breakfast discussing the events at the Ball and the harrowing rescue of her sister. She wished herself anywhere but there, lest her struggle be transparent and she dampen the mood. Uncharitably, she wondered how long her parents would wish to remain in Scotland.

When she could suffer through no more, she excused herself from the table and escaped to the rose garden. Plucking a fragrant white bloom, she paced back and forth along the gravel path, tearing the petals away in an agitation of indecision.

"What am I to do? I should tell him…I should not. I should tell him…I should not."

"The poor rose," she heard Yardley remark. She turned to face him, and he was leaning against the gate looking devilishly handsome.

"I suppose it is in the eye of the beholder. I think roses are just as lovely strewn about in petals."

She looked down at the last petal in her hand, trying to work up her courage. But then she took another look at him and decided to wait. She wanted him to choose her freely.

"I have come to take my leave. I have a long journey ahead and I must take advantage of the clear skies whilst I may."

"So, we have come back to discussing the weather," she quipped.

He laughed. "It seems we have."

"Thank you," she began to say, but suddenly he was standing in front of her.

"There is no need to thank me. Jolie, I..." He hesitated as their eyes met, and Margaux and Lord Craig walked out onto the nearby terrace.

Jolie sighed.

"I wish you well. I hope I may call on you again some time," Yardley said with sincerity. "I have something for you to read on your journey." He held out three volumes of a book entitled *Pride and Prejudice*.

"Yes, of course. Thank you, and Godspeed on your journey."

He gave her a quick bow and walked toward the stables. She smiled briefly at Margaux and Lord Craig, then hurried inside to find somewhere to be alone again.

Jolie watched from the parlour window as Yardley rode away down the drive. She stood looking out long after he had disappeared through the trees, and she felt anger and anguish at the same time.

"He left me," she said out loud in disbelief. "He left me."

And he had left to go after his former wife. An irritating tear dripped from her cheek and she swept it away with frustration.

She did not want to be a lovesick fool, but she was the biggest fool of all. She forced herself away from the window. When she turned, her mother was standing at the doorway looking sympathetic.

She wanted to put on a cheerful face and pretend she was unaffected, but she went to her *maman* and wept in her arms.

"I have lost him."

"Did you ever have him?" Lady Ashbury asked.

"I refused him. Now it is too late." It was so much more than those simple words.

"It does not appear that all hope is lost," her mother said with understanding.

"But he left to go after his former wife."

"*Je suis désolé , ma chere,*" her mother said, trying to comfort her. "Do you wish to return to London? The Duchess is returning, and we told Yardley we would accompany her."

Jolie nodded. Watching Margaux in love was not the medicine she needed at the moment. Margaux would sense Jolie's hurt and be unable to be as happy with her new husband. Yes, London would be the best place to drown in her misery. "I think it would be best. Margaux and Lord Craig need time alone together."

"*Oui.* We shall depart soon, *non?*"

"*S'il vous plait,*" Jolie whispered.

"I shall see to arranging things as quickly as possible," her mother said, as she kissed her daughter on the head and walked out of the room.

Jolie dried her eyes and walked back to the garden to speak with Margaux. She had been deliberately obtuse about Yardley when she had talked to her before the Ball, and felt she should confess to her sister before leaving.

Margaux and Lord Craig were still in the garden, sitting close together on a bench, her head on his shoulder. Jolie felt her throat tighten and tears threaten, and she had to take a moment to compose herself. She was becoming a watering pot of late!

"May I interrupt? We are to head back to England today, so I wanted a few moments with Margaux."

"So soon?" Margaux asked.

"The two of you need some time alone together," she explained.

Lord Craig, who had risen to his feet at Jolie's approach, then interposed. "I will leave you alone to talk to your sister." He smiled lovingly at his wife and bowed to Jolie.

"Thank you," Jolie said as she took his place on the bench.

Margaux clasped her hand. "I do not want you to leave," she said. Tears filled her eyes.

"When you have had time to become properly acquainted with your husband you will see more of me than you wish. You have had a strange start to your marriage, but I think your affections are engaged now?"

Margaux nodded. "It will never be the same again though, will it? I am married, you soon will be."

Jolie interrupted. "No."

"Whatever do you mean? I saw the two of you together. You cannot fool me. He is different than the others you have denied. I have never seen you in love before. And you are in love, are you not? You cannot deny it to me."

"I do not." Jolie struggled to speak as tears streamed down her face. "I have lost him."

Margaux hugged her. "I cannot believe it," she exclaimed. "Did you exchange cross words before he departed?"

"No, and that is the problem. He left to go and see to his former wife. Those are not the actions of a man in love with me. I thought...and I was going to tell him...but I decided it would be best if he came to me."

"Perhaps you are correct. Men do like to exert themselves in this matter. If you gave him all indications his suit would be welcome, you have nothing to fear. Perhaps he needs to tidy up his affairs before offering."

Jolie could feel the blood rush from her head.

"Jolie? What is it?"

She bit her lip and shook her head. "I am a fool." She stood and straightened her skirts to avoid looking into her sister's eyes. "Please do write often. I want to know everything. We shall make plans to visit very soon."

"You are going to leave without telling me? I know that you are upset. Please, Jolie."

"It is a very long, unfortunate tale."

"I have time," Margaux said.

Jolie sat back down on the bench.

"In summation, he offered for me via his solicitor before we had been introduced. I refused him most colourfully, of which he has frequently reminded me since. Then unbeknownst to either of us, we were thrown together constantly by Easton and Elly. We returned to Wyndham, due to Uncle's poor health, and he escorted me here because he had little choice. That is the end of the tale, with no happy-ever-after."

"Oh, Jolie."

"There is nothing else to say is there? I utterly botched it."

"It is certainly more complicated than I had supposed. However, I do

174

not think all is lost. I agree you should return and let him know of your changed feelings. Would you not forever regret not having told him and be wondering? The worst that can happen is he says no."

"Which seems worse than I can bear," she whispered.

"One day at a time, dear sister. It is how I have managed."

Jolie nodded. "I will remember that."

They stood and walked together around to the front drive. The carriages were loaded and the others were waiting. Jolie kissed her sister on the cheek. *"Au revoir, ma sœur."*

~*~

Benedict felt heartsick as he led his horse through the gates of Castle Craig, for he did not know what the outcome of his relationship with Beaujolais would be. He felt certain her opinion of him had changed—she was brimming with passion and stirred his blood, as even Lillian had not. She had nearly forgotten herself entirely when she had kissed him, and so had he. The words she had uttered while tearing the rose apart were a vivid memory. She had been trying to decide whether or not to speak with him. If they had not been interrupted he would have likely thrown all of his scruples to the ground with her petals.

Before Beaujolais had entered his life, Benedict had felt little emotion beyond anger or pain in the past decade. Laughing aloud, he reminisced about their tumultuous courtship, and it was a courtship, whether or not she realised it. She was not afraid of him as most females appeared to be, and though he was terrified of his attraction to her, of losing himself again, he felt her to be worth the risk. When precisely had he decided he must marry this woman and give up on a business arrangement? When had she become essential to a happy future? Probably the first moment he saw her atop Hector.

As the days seemed to grow longer in the saddle, he began to grow melancholic. He rode as hard as possible to keep his mind from wandering to his misery. For Beaujolais was not yet his, and might never be. Several times, he had almost asked for her hand again impulsively, but her concern for her sister had stopped him. On further reflection, he had realised he must resolve the situation with Lillian before subjecting Beaujolais to potential scandal. For he knew there was little likelihood the situation would resolve quietly or with expediency, especially if Fairmont and Hughes' instincts were correct about Lillian and Dannon's illegal doings. The papers would eat him for supper, and it was likely some or all of those involved would never recover—if they made it out alive.

He stopped again at his Yardley estate on the way to London, in order to gather any necessary items and business before spending an interminable time in London. He could not bring himself to enter his favourite room and play the pianoforte for fear he would lose courage and return to her. The room would still hold her scent and the sound of her song would stay in his mind.

Instead, he went to his study to review his estate business, knowing Hughes had not attended to it in his absence on the Continent. Fortunately, there were few items that needed immediate attention, and he addressed them with expedience in order to leave for London as soon as possible. When he had tidied up the correspondence and authorised necessary payments and repairs, he looked through the more personal letters.

An anonymous parcel contained one of the broadsheets, folded with a caricature prominently displayed. It was much as he would have suspected

There was a drawing of a man's head, resembling Dannon's, was depicted inside a package with the Yardley Ducal seal upon it and addressed to Lord Fairmont. It was captioned: *For overseas delivery.*

He slammed his fist down on the desk, he threw the paper across the room and dropped his head in his hands. If the scandalmongers already knew he had sent Dannon to Fairmont, there was little chance Dannon and Lillian could be got rid of quietly. This was going to be worse than he had anticipated.

He slept fitfully and arose with the first crow of the cock, and rode into London later the next day. He chose to take Dido, for she had failed to come into foal. He could not bring himself to ride Hector, for the memories of Jolie atop him were too raw.

Chapter Nineteen

If Jolie thought the journey to Scotland had been long, the way back was an eternity. She had been unable to read, either because the Duchess was chatty, or the roads were too poor. Her mother and the Duchess had become fast friends, and the burden of entertaining the Duchess had been alleviated to a great degree by her mother. The relief Jolie felt when they arrived in London was great. The false façade of happiness she had worn for several weeks fell away; she developed a case of the dismals, for she had neither seen nor had word from Yardley since their parting in the garden at Craig Castle.

The Season was now over, and Jolie was thankful to have time to sulk in the privacy of her room. She spied the volumes of *Pride and Prejudice* Yardley had given her, but which she had barely opened. Rain was beating against the window panes and the skies were leaden. A brisk wind howled down the chimneys and whistled under the eaves. Until the weather turned, she was forced to forgo the joys of walking and feeding the birds. She took the first book in the set and, curling up in the window seat, opened the cover.

To Beaujolais,
May you find this diverting and enlightening,
Ever yours,
Benedict

She breathed a sigh of relief, and felt a glimmer of hope. She read along for a time, thinking of how she had thought Yardley insufferable and proud, in the same way Lizzy felt about Darcy.

"Perhaps she misjudges him," Jolie said out loud.

My good opinion once lost is lost forever.

She gasped.

"Could it be? It would be uncanny." She continued on.

There are none handsome enough to tempt me.

"I cannot believe it of him! Yardley, a novel reader?" She recalled how he had woven the brilliant lines into conversation. Elly had once exclaimed the virtues of this authoress and her wit.

"He was toying with me. How stupid he must think me."

She became fully engrossed in the story from that point onwards. Reading every line made her feel closer to him, and perhaps she might one day benefit by showing her own prowess through recitation of the authoress's words.

She read on through the night, and finally slept after she saw the words '*The End*' through tired eyes and with an aching head.

She dreamt that night, or early that morning, of her own happy ending, where Lillian and Dannon were forced to flee in shame, and Yardley confessed his love and ardour for her alone.

Her renewed hope was not to last long. Later in the day, she ventured forth to the *modiste*, and met Madame Clement the moment she entered the small establishment littered with fabrics and patterns.

"Bonjour, Mademoiselle Winslow. You recall Madame Clement? She has been gracious enough to assist me with new designs," Madame Monique remarked as she indicated some drawings of fashion plates.

"*Oui, bien sûr. Bonjour,*" Madame Clement said as civilly as she could manage, and bobbed a very shallow curtsy.

"*Pardonnez-moi,* we are very disturbed this morning. My assistant,

Jemima, has gone missing," Madame Monique explained.

"Oh dear. You are certain?" Jolie asked in disbelief.

"*Oui.* She lives upstairs and has not been home for two days. It is unlike her. I am afraid she has become one of the victims of this mad person."

"This mad person?" Jolie echoed.

"Many young girls have gone missing recently. They believe there is someone kidnapping them."

Jolie felt sick, and afraid. "Have you told anyone?" she enquired.

"Who am I to tell? She has no family to run to," the seamstress said hopelessly, wringing her hands on the muslin she held in her hands.

"You could hire a Runner," Jolie suggested.

"It would be above my touch," the *modiste* said sadly.

"Would you like me to inform my father? If you tell me everything you can remember of Jemima, perhaps he might assist you. She was the pretty one with auburn hair who fitted my riding habit, was she not?" Jolie asked.

"*Oui,* that was Jemima," Madame Monique said wiping tears from her cheeks. "It is most kind of you to help, mademoiselle."

The entire time Jolie was conversing with Madame Monique, Madame Clement remained silent, and Jolie felt anxious to depart. Her instinct was warning her to be careful around the woman.

"I will send word after I speak with my father."

"*Merci,* mademoiselle."

Jolie hurried to the carriage with her maid and directed the coachman to hasten home. She might have led a sheltered life, but she had overheard her brother mention things about young girls and how brothels would enslave them. Poor, innocent Jemima, with no family to look out for her! How many victims were missing from slums for whom there were no resources for helping to find them? She felt shaken, and wanted to try to help.

She alighted from the carriage almost before the vehicle had stopped, and asked after her father.

"He is in his study, Lady Beaujolais," the butler replied. "But this was just now delivered for you."

"*Merci*, Arnaud," Jolie replied as she took the letter from the butler and walked on.

"Papa!" she exclaimed when she entered her father's study. "I need your help. Madame Monique's assistant has gone missing."

Her father raised his eyebrows as he looked up from his desk and sat back in his chair.

"It is true," she exclaimed. "I was just at the *modiste's*, and Madame Monique was distraught. She says Jemima has not come home for two days. That sweet young girl has helped me before. She has no family she would have returned to," Jolie explained.

Her father sat thinking for a while before responding. "I suppose you have heard that several girls have gone missing?"

"I have heard it mentioned. I want to try to help this girl who has no one to look for her. Can you hire a Runner?" she pleaded.

"I do not know, Jolie. We cannot help everyone."

"But, *Papa*! That is not like you. I will pay with my own money if that is the issue."

He sighed and pinched the bridge of his nose. "That will not be necessary. I will go speak with one today. Can you give me a good description of the girl?"

Jolie proceeded to describe Jemima as best she could. But something was still disturbing her and she mentioned it to her father.

"*Papa*, when I was at the *modiste*, Madame Clement was also there."

"Yardley's former wife?" he asked with surprise.

Jolie nodded.

"Was she unkind to you?"

"No. It is not that. But I had a bad feeling the entire time I was near her. She was silent and seemed strange while Madame Monique was telling me about Jemima."

"Perhaps your feelings for Yardley are clouding your judgement. It is nothing we can prosecute Madame Clement for."

Jolie felt her cheeks blush. She should not be surprised that her father knew about her feelings for Yardley. Her mother was never one to keep secrets from him.

"I will see what I can do. Can you also give me the *modiste's* direction if they wish to speak with her?"

"Thank you, oh, thank you, *Papa*!" Jolie said, as she threw her arms around her father.

"What have you there?" Lord Ashbury indicated her letter.

"I do not know. Arnaud only now handed it to me."

"Open it. It might be from Margaux or Anjou."

"I do not believe so. There is no post or frank," she said inspecting the outside. She slid her finger under the seal and gasped as she looked inside.

"What is the matter, dear?" her father asked with concern and moved to see the note.

It was the dreadful cartoon that had been drawn after the come-out, except in this copy Jolie had been torn from Yardley and Lillian.

"I collect this is meant to be a veiled threat of some sort," her father remarked.

"I do not understand," Jolie said in disbelief.

"Likely a jealous rival. Leave it to me and do not worry," he said, as he took it from her hands. "Did Arnaud say who delivered it? Never mind, it was likely a street urchin. No one delivers their own threat themselves," he reasoned aloud.

~*~

Benedict was sitting in Lord Fairmont's library with Hughes. For perhaps the dozenth time, they were debating how to trap Dannon, and, potentially, Lillian. They had been following both of them for weeks now, without any concrete proof they were involved in something nefarious.

There was a knock at the door, and the butler entered when acknowledged.

"Lord Ashbury is here to see you, my lord."

"Ashbury?" Yardley looked at the others, who shook their heads. "Send him in."

"Good afternoon, Fairmont, Yardley. I called at your house and was informed you were here. I hope you do not mind the intrusion, but Jolie felt I should seek help about another girl who has gone missing from her *modiste's*," Lord Ashbury explained.

Suddenly Benedict was all interest. He did not know the Ashburys were returned to London, although his mother had sent word she was in town. Had Ashbury's daughter returned also?

"I remember you mentioning it before we left Scotland as being one of your reasons for your early departure."

Benedict gave a nod in acknowledgement. "Jolie mentioned today that Madame Clement was present at the *modiste's*, and she felt as if the lady was acting strangely. I do not know if there is a connection, but Jolie asked me to employ a Runner to find the girl named Jemima."

Benedict's heart raced, knowing Beaujolais was in town.

"Does the girl fit the description of the others who have gone missing?" Fairmont asked.

"To the best of my knowledge," Ashbury replied. "She was not above eighteen years of age, very handsome, and had no family to seek her."

Fairmont muttered an oath and slammed his fist against the desk. "We must stop this," he exclaimed.

"We should bring Lord Ashbury in on our suspicions. Perhaps we are missing an obvious piece of the puzzle he might be able to see," Benedict reasoned.

Fairmont cocked his head in agreement.

"Go ahead, Hughes."

"Thus far, we only have suspicions based on past knowledge of Madame Clement and Lord Dannon. I went to France to ascertain why they had suddenly appeared in England. I was able to surmise they left France in a hurry, and Monsieur Clement had died under suspicious circumstances. The bank accounts of all parties had been emptied. All were known to keep rather low company in Paris, but that was expected. When my return vessel was detoured to Jersey, I overheard some drunken locals speaking of Dannon. It is suspected he is running an elite brothel there, but the place is guarded better than Newgate. The timing of their arrival in England, together with the disappearance of the missing girls, is too coincidental. We have had Madame Clement trailed since we discovered Dannon following Yardley and Lady Beaujolais on their way to Scotland."

Lord Ashbury interrupted. "Why was I not told of this?"

"I thought it had been dealt with, and I supposed the object of his scheme was me. Lillian has already asked for funds, but she refused to accept them on my terms. I was hardly in Scotland long enough to recollect the matter, with everything else that occurred."

"Fair enough," Ashbury conceded. "Please proceed."

"The only discovery we have made whilst following Madame Clement is that she spends a great deal of time at *modistes* and milliners. Last night, Lord Dannon escaped our surveillance. We believe he may have left England."

"Is there anything suspect about a female being in either place? My wife and daughters keep several in business single-handedly," Ashbury said sardonically.

"But do they visit every day? It seems extraordinary, but we have found nothing to indicate wrong-doing," Hughes said with disgust.

"What else is there to do, but follow?" Ashbury asked.

"We have sent Runners to Paris and to Jersey to investigate further. We are continuing to follow Madame Clement. Until we catch either of them with the girls, or taking one, there is little we can do."

"I am tired of waiting. This could go on indefinitely," Benedict said with frustration.

"What do you suggest? We lay a trap? That could endanger an innocent victim," Fairmont chimed in.

"And Lillian and Dannon are cunning. It would be difficult to deceive them. Yet how many girls will go missing while we decide?" Benedict asked.

"I will send for the Runners working on this case. You may let them know of Jemima's disappearance, and perhaps they will provide some more clues," Fairmont decided, and rang for a footman.

It was some time before the head of the Bow Street court himself arrived, with Mr Peters, the man whom Ashbury had hired to search for the Mulligans in Scotland.

"Sir John, very good of you to come," Fairmont said.

"I thought it best to update you myself. This has to be stopped quickly. This is Mr Peters, one of my best Runners."

"I am familiar with Mr Peters," Lord Ashbury said. "He helped us with another matter."

"Indeed," Sir John remarked. He was blind but very astute. Based on his mannerisms, it was difficult to tell he was unable to see.

"We spoke to Madame Monique after we received your note earlier, Ashbury. It appears as if all of the missing girls are from the area of the affluent shops. They were employed as assistants at milliners, *modistes*, and there is one from a bakery. All were near Oxford and Bond Street. That is what makes it more extraordinary. Sadly, if we were discussing Seven Dials or Saint Giles, it would be commonplace. This makes six girls within one month and I will not tolerate it! Now, what have you got for me? I assume you did not call us in merely over this seamstress?" Sir John asked.

Fairmont spoke. "No, Sir John, we fear we know who the perpetrators are. However, we have no proof."

Sir John narrowed his eyes. "Please elaborate," he said with interest.

"We believe Lord Dannon and Madame Clement, formally known to you as Lillian Stanton, Countess Langdon, to be responsible."

"I see. I knew you had hired Runners to have them followed, but I was led to believe it was because of a different matter."

"It began that way, yes," Benedict explained. "It was only after the revelation that Dannon is purported to be running an expensive bordello from the island of Jersey, together with the missing girls, that we began to suspect. Lillian appeared unexpectedly and wanted money. So I sent Hughes to Paris to determine why they had suddenly reappeared in England. He discovered they left France in haste, and Monsieur Clement's death was suspicious. None of it adds up."

"It certainly bears looking into, as I have no other leads," Sir John agreed. "I do not think I would have made the connection myself for some time."

"Unfortunately, we may be wrong, and Dannon made a generous donation to the royal coffers to gain Prinny's acceptance," Fairmont lamented.

"We also believe Dannon may have taken the girls to Jersey. He managed to escape our man last evening," Hughes added.

"Peters, I believe we should send more men to Jersey to assist. I will step up the presence of men in Oxford and Bond Streets," Sir Johns said to Peters.

"Do you think we should lay a trap?" Benedict asked.

Sir John was silent a few moments while he considered the question. He finally answered. "No. We need more information, first. The connection is new to me and I must think on it before acting."

Benedict could respect his discretion. However, he was growing impatient.

Sir John stood. "If you hear anything further, please send word."

Sir John and Peters took their leave.

Hughes remained standing. "I think I should return to Jersey myself, Your Grace. We do not know what they plan to do with the girls."

"I want the blackguard caught. I will go with you, Hughes," Fairmont declared.

"I will assist in following Lillian. Perhaps I might be able to gather more information under the pretence I am shopping for my sister," Benedict suggested.

"Perhaps," Ashbury suggested. "My wife and daughter might be able to do the same. They are quite at ease with spending money."

"I do not want Lady Beaujolais involved," Benedict said in a commanding tone.

Ashbury looked astounded. "Do you think she is in danger?"

"*Hell hath no fury like a woman scorned*. Lillian suspects there is something between your daughter and myself. She might decide to manipulate me at Lady Beaujolais' expense."

"Good God," Ashbury exclaimed. He pulled the cartoon that had been delivered to Jolie earlier from his pocket and handed it to Benedict. "Do you think this is a threat?"

Benedict sighed in frustration. "I received the same thing. It was waiting for me at Yardley when I first returned. I did not realise it was aimed at her. I thought it from Lillian or Dannon."

"Let me know what I may do to help," Ashbury said with quiet concern.

"For now, keep your daughter safe and far away from me."

Chapter Twenty

The Duchess of Yardley joined Jolie and her mother for a light tea in the parlour that same afternoon. The two elder ladies chatted comfortably while nibbling on slices of bread and butter, slivers of ham and small cakes. Her father having not yet returned from visiting the Runners, Jolie was distracted and paid little heed to their conversation.

"It is becoming tiresome in town. Perhaps we should hold a soiree," Lady Ashbury suggested to the Duchess.

"There is no one in town to *soiree* with, and Charlotte is happy in the country with Lady Olivia," the Duchess commiserated. "There must be a way to bring our pitiful offspring together."

"I suppose we could hold a dinner," Lady Ashbury said, disappointment colouring her voice.

She heard a door close, drawing her attention back to the moment. As she gathered the gist of the conversation, Jolie was for once thankful for the *ton's* summer exodus to the country.

When her father entered the parlour, she practically leapt from her seat.

"Have you any news?"

"Very little, I'm afraid. It does seem they suspect the girls are being used for ill-purpose. There is some suspicion Lord Dannon is involved, but that is only a theory, mind you."

"Dannon? Is that not the scoundrel I discovered trying to sneak into your room at the inn?" the Duchess demanded of Jolie.

"The very one. I was only informed about the incident by Yardley this afternoon," Lord Ashbury answered with a pointed look at his daughter.

"You saw Yardley?" Jolie asked with surprise.

"I did. I went to him first after sending a note to Bow Street. I found him at Lord Fairmont's house, discussing the problem with him. This is a much deeper situation than I imagined. The head of the Bow Street court came to speak to us."

"Dear me," Lady Ashbury said.

"In addition, I discovered that Yardley was sent a copy of the cartoon, also torn in two," he said gravely.

"What cartoon?" Lady Ashbury and the Duchess asked simultaneously.

"It was the caricature of Yardley caught by the arms between Madame Clement and Jolie after Olivia and Charlotte's début."

"What can it mean?" Jolie wondered out loud.

"It might mean simple jealousy. However, Yardley feels you might be in some danger and should keep your distance from him."

"Is that why he has not called?" she asked hopefully.

"Very likely."

"That hussy, Lillian, was not content with Benedict, yet, she cannot abide anyone else having him either," the Duchess observed acidly.

"I do not understand how Madame Clement and Lord Dannon are connected," Lady Ashbury said, still confused.

"Dannon was involved in the scandal that ruined Benedict's marriage," the Duchess explained.

"Dannon and Madame Clement have been seen together since they returned," Jolie added.

"And the girls have gone missing since their return here," Ashbury said. "It is interesting that Lord Dannon and Madame Clement's reappearance on these shores has coincided with the spate of missing girls, but it is no surety of their involvement."

"What does Sir John mean to do about it?" the Duchess asked.

"Fairmont and Hughes are departing for Jersey, where Dannon is thought to be running a house of ill repute, and is the likely destination of these poor girls, I regret to say. Yardley is to stay and keep an eye on Lillian, whom they believe is luring the girls away."

"I suggested, my dear, you and your mother, might help the cause by doing a little extra shopping and taking note of anything of interest you may observe. Yardley, however, insisted I keep you safe."

"I do not see what the harm would be if I am not alone," Jolie insisted.

"*Oui*. I will go with her. I have a sharp eye," the Marchioness stated.

"I, too, am able to help. I need a few bonnets and gloves for Charlotte," the Duchess said with an arch look.

"Very well, but do be careful. I am not even certain what you should be looking for," he said with a frown.

"Your Grace, do you see your son soon?" Jolie asked impetuously.

"I am to dine with him this night," she replied.

"Would it be impertinent then, for me to ask you to deliver a letter to him?"

"I do not mind if it is, my dear. I shall be happy to deliver it for you into his hands."

Jolie smiled. "I shall write a note at once and return on the instant."

Jolie had an idea, but she did not know if Yardley would agree to it.

Dear Yardley, she wrote.

I have been apprised of the situation by my father, He says you fear for my safety. While I do not fully comprehend your reasoning, , I will defer to your judgement (on this occasion at least). I do believe I may be of

191

assistance, but the plan hinges on a minor detail. May I be so bold as to enquire if you have already asked someone to be your wife? If not, I should wish to arrange a meeting to discuss my plan.

Kind regards,

Beaujolais

She hurried back to the Duchess, and gave the letter into her safekeeping. She waited for a reply, which she hoped would be quickly forthcoming, if for no other reason than Yardley's curiosity would be piqued. She had little time to forge her plan and think of a way to convince him.

There was a knock on the door within half an hour, which Jolie thought was rather prompt, even for Yardley. However, when Arnaud handed her the note, she opened it eagerly; however, the words which met her avid gaze had not come from the Duke.

Mind your own business and watch your step. I am.

Jolie's breath caught in her throat. Now she truly was afraid. She ran to the door.

"Arnaud?"

"Yes, my lady?"

"Who delivered this?"

"A street urchin," he said distastefully.

"As I suspected. Thank you."

He bowed, and she went back into the parlour.

Should she inform her mother and father? Should she send a second note to Yardley? If she told them, they would lock her away until this was over, which was not to be thought of. She swiftly folded the letter away and hid it in her reticule.

There was another knock, and this time Arnaud handed her the note she was waiting for.

Lady Beaujolais,

While I am flattered you take such an interest in my affairs, the answer to your question is negative. But I regret to inform you we cannot meet for the time being.

Yours, etc.,

Yardley

"Insufferable oaf!" she exclaimed as she marched over to the escritoire.

Your Grace,

You shall honour me with an audience even if it requires me to call on you!

Affectionately,

Lady Beaujolais

She paced the parquet floor whilst she awaited his reply, which was short and succinct: *No.*

She penned another curt reply:

I shall be there at ten of the clock.

The next reply came more quickly than the last:

You shall do no such thing. Await my summons and I will arrange
something.

Jolie smiled. Her heart sang, and she realised how she had missed him.
Perhaps he was not so disagreeable after all.

~*~

If Lillian did not beat him to it, Benedict would wring Beaujolais'
exquisite neck and thus save himself any further trouble. If she
understood the situation, why was she putting herself at risk? Having
given the matter a good deal of thought, he had sent her a note detailing
the plan. It seemed unlikely they would be followed into the open; in that
eventuality, however, he hoped and deemed the chances of their being
harmed to be reduced. He waited on the bench where Beaujolais liked to
feed the birds near the Serpentine every day.

Various officers of the law were stationed in inconspicuous positions
around the park, in case there should be trouble.

"I think someone followed me here," Beaujolais said nervously when
she saw him, then burst out laughing.

"You dislike my disguise?" Benedict said in mock offence.

"It is hideous," she said frankly.

He had attempted to dress as a footman in livery, wig and all.

"And you are supposed to be a scullery maid? Promise me you will
never wear a mob-cap again," he said, eyeing the ridiculous headwear
with distaste. "Kindly inform me why we must meet when the danger is
so great?" he asked tersely.

"Do you truly believe they mean to harm me? Madame Clement does
not seem a lunatic to me."

"Oh, she is quite sane. However, that does not mean she is not dangerous. Lillian gets what Lillian wants."

"But what does she want?"

"That is precisely what I do not know, and it is why you are in danger."

"Clearly, she does not want me to have you."

"And does that bother you?" he asked, fishing for a minnow of encouragement.

Evading his question she said, "I think it is none of her concern whether I have you or not. She gave you up."

"Indeed. Do you not miss me even a little?" he prodded hopefully.

"Perhaps a very little." She held up her thumb and forefinger with a scant amount of space between them to indicate how much.

He tried not to smile. He was more determined than ever to see the backside of Lillian and Dannon.

"Please enlighten me of your brilliant plan."

"It seems rather silly now that I have to tell it to someone," she said, worrying her lower lip, drawing his eyes to fixate on the full, pink curve and held him spellbound.

"Now I am intrigued. Do go on." He flicked his wrist in encouragement.

She blushed and there was a twinge in his heart.

"Very well, I thought we could announce our engagement."

His mouth must have gaped open. He was stunned.

"I beg your pardon?"

"It made perfect sense to me last night," she said, frowning, then looking down at her boots. "I thought it would give me the perfect excuse to be frequenting the shops. And I thought it might anger Madame Clement enough to misstep."

She was now pacing in circles as she spoke. It took every bit of Benedict's self-control not to take her in his arms and taste her lips. It had been too long. He firmed his resolve with difficulty.

"But I did not ask."

Her head lifted and her eyes sparked. He could watch this all day.

"But you did," she insisted.

"Are you referring to the time when you said you would rather rot in hell then marry me?"

"A gentleman would not mention it," she said, clearly fuming, one fist balled up at her side and her chin lifted at a belligerent angle.

He was enjoying himself greatly. "You did not *permit me to tell you how ardently I love and admire you.*"

She gave him a look of exasperation. "Very clever. I know not if you are in earnest or jest." She turned to walk away and he caught her arm.

"Jolie, wait. I am in earnest, even if expressed it poorly. I do not think you can have thought this through. If we announce our betrothal, there will be no crying off afterwards." He looked deep into her eyes. He loved this woman more than he had ever loved anyone before. Please let her not be planning this as a ruse.

"I realise that," she said, not taking her gaze away from his.

He sucked in his breath. Was he finally hearing the words he longed to hear? Then reality struck. They could not be free to love each other until they were rid of Lillian, and likely Dannon as well.

He pulled her to him for a brief kiss, knocking his wig askew.

She giggled. "Your wig is tickling me."

He pulled back with exasperation. "Woman, if we were married, I would carry you back to the house and punish you for your impertinence," he said with false severity.

"Next to being married, a girl likes to be crossed in love a little now and then," she replied with a pert grin.

"Touché. I am glad to know my wit has not been for naught," he said, as he shook his head and took her arm. "Let us return to Ashbury Court. We need to make plans to shop for your bridal raiment."

"I believe we need to put a notice in the papers for the morning," she said, thinking out loud as they walked.

"I'll have Hughes see to it." He stopped. "Bother!" he exclaimed. "Hughes is on his way to Jersey."

"I am certain we can manage something satisfactory between all of us at Ashbury. Come along, my dear sir."

Yardley discreetly indicated to the men standing watch that they should follow along.

Chapter Twenty-One

Jolie and Yardley arrived at her father's house looking ridiculous in ill-fitting servant's costumes. His face a mask of frosty haughtiness, Arnaud had forbid them entry and was about to close the door in their faces until Jolie pulled the mob-cap from her head.

She smiled, and though he looked affronted, Arnaud let them enter.

"Would you request my parents to join us in the parlour?" Jolie asked.

"I would also like to have a note delivered to the Duchess of Yardley," Benedict stated.

"Very good, your Grace. I will have a footman awaiting your convenience."

"I will go and change my dress while you write to your mother. Then we may explain what this is all about once we are all together," Jolie said, as she showed him to the desk where he could find what he needed to pen a note.

When they had all assembled after nuncheon, and Yardley had received Lord Ashbury's permission, he and Jolie shared the news with their mothers.

"I knew it!" Lady Ashbury exclaimed, as she went over to her future son-in-law, and allowed him to kiss her hand.

"I say it is about time," was the Duchess's response. "I suppose that the news was worth being aroused at an ungodly hour for."

"Does this have anything to do with Madame Clement?" Lady Ashbury asked pointedly.

"Perhaps it encouraged us to proceed," Jolie responded.

"But we both desire it, nonetheless," Benedict reassured her.

"We hope it will encourage her to make a mistake if she is involved," Jolie explained.

"She always was a jealous one," the Duchess confirmed.

"It may have an effect. However, I anticipate the news might make her realise the Yardley coffers will henceforth be closed to her."

"Mark my words, she will find a way to try and blackmail you," the Duchess prophesied.

"She will have to deal with me first," Jolie announced defiantly. "Let us forge a plan. I am ready to carry on with our lives."

"Hear, hear," Benedict agreed.

"We will send notices to all of the papers," Lady Ashbury, mistress of planning, stated eagerly.

"That will ruffle her feathers for certain," the Duchess said with a wry smile.

"We can then shop for my trousseau."

"Will that be enough to lure Madame Clement?" Lord Ashbury wondered doubtfully.

"If I am there with Jolie, I believe it will. As we are all at the shops, we can begin to ask questions. I have a feeling the shopkeepers will be more open with us than they have been with the Runners."

"I had not thought of it, but I suspect you are correct."

"I advise everyone to take a full purse," he advised. "I've yet to meet anyone of the working class who could afford to remain mum when a crown was sitting in front of them. Shall I come for you in two hours?" he asked Jolie. "I would prefer to wear my own clothes," he said with one of his rare, sheepish grins.

~*~

"Good afternoon, my future Duchess, fair," Benedict greeted Jolie

199

later that afternoon when she walked into the parlour.

"Good afternoon," she replied, forcing a smile she did not feel. Should she tell him about the note she had just received from Lillian?

"What is it, Jolie?" He took her hands and looked into her eyes.

She hesitated.

"Please tell me you are not having second thoughts, because the notice appeared in every paper in the kingdom this morning."

"No. I am not regretting the betrothal," she reassured him.

"Then tell me what is bothering you. Let us have no secrets between us."

She pulled the note from her dress and handed it to him.

You did not heed my warnings. You will regret it.

"You are not to leave this house," Benedict commanded. He began to pace the room in anger.

"Do not be a tyrant," Jolie replied, with a raised voice.

"I am a tyrant because I love you and want to protect you?" he asked in disbelief.

"You love me?"

He sighed in exasperation, and ran his fingers through his hair. "You are going to be the death of me."

She stepped close to him and began to smooth his hair back into place.

"Nonsense. As long as you do not presume to lord it over me we will get along splendidly."

"Shall I escort you to Lillian, then?" he asked sardonically.

"In a manner of speaking, yes. But this has become personal and I intend to see that she is brought to account. We will go to the *modiste* as planned. I expect she will arrive shortly after we do, if she is following us as she appears to be."

"And what shall we do about it?"

"We shall ask her where she has taken the girls," Jolie said plainly.

"And you think she will confess?" Benedict asked derisively.

"Unlikely, but she may not know that we know she is involved in the kidnappings. I believe she is growing anxious, and if Dannon is not here to back her up, she may not be so strong."

"You certainly believe many things," he rejoined. "And I would remind you that we do not know where Dannon is."

"I imagine she will lead us to him."

"Perhaps. Very well." He reluctantly agreed to her plan. "I shall first send a note to Peters and Sir John at Bow Street to let them know.

She put on her bonnet and gathered her reticule, while Yardley penned a note to the Runners.

Her mother and the Duchess joined them in the entrance hall and they walked outside to the waiting barouche. A groom was holding Dido for Yardley to ride. She watched him strap a pistol to the front of the saddle, and her heart gave a lurch at the danger they faced.

They rode to the *modiste's* shop only a few streets away. Yardley handed the horse to an urchin to hold, and he helped her alight as Lady Ashbury and the Duchess went around the corner to a silk warehouse.

They entered the small shop, and Madame Monique hurried over to them.

"Congratulations, mademoiselle," she effused.

"*Merci,*" Jolie responded. She offered the dressmaker a pleasant smile.

"Do you have any news of Jemima? I shall have to replace her soon if she is not found. I simply cannot keep up with the work. I do thank you for sending the Runners to me. How may I properly thank you? You are here for your bridal clothes, *non*? I will give you some special lace for it."

"That is not necessary, Madame. I do appreciate the sentiment, but we have not found Jemima yet."

"We are here for whatever Lady Beaujolais' heart desires," Yardley interjected.

Madame smiled. "Do you have any preferences, *Monsieur le Duc*?"

"Only to see my bride happy," he replied.

"Very well, I have a new silk and some new Parisian lace for your gown," she said to Jolie.

Madame led Jolie away to the next room to show her fabrics, and Madame Clement entered the shop.

Yardley said curtly through clenched teeth, "Lillian."

"Benedict. Why are you here?" Madame Clement said in a tone of astonishment.

"I imagine you know very well. I am helping my betrothed select her wardrobe. Are you not going to congratulate us?"

"I do not care whom you choose to make a miserable duchess, as long as it is not me," she snarled.

"Do you not? Then would you kindly refrain from sending threats to Lady Beaujolais?"

"I do not know what you mean," she said, feigning innocence, though her eyes were narrowed.

"Let us not play coy, Lillian. What have you done with the girls?"

"What girls do you refer to?" she asked evasively.

"The girls who have been kidnapped from the shops on this street. I know you are involved."

"No one was taken against their will. They were offered a better life and chose to take it."

Jolie and Madame Monique were listening to the conversation and both gasped at the admission.

"Go and find Mr Peters at Bow Street. Quickly!" Jolie said in a whisper to Madame Monique.

The seamstress nodded and sneaked out of the back door.

"What better life would you be referring to? One where men abuse them and demand they serve their every whim? One where saying no is not allowed? You disgust me, Lillian."

Lillian seethed with rage as her face turned red and a vein pulsed at her temple. "You think your little ice princess will satisfy your needs?" She cackled hysterically.

"Enough! You had your chance and you chose to destroy it."

Jolie was furious. She wanted to strangle the woman herself. She looked around the small dressing room for something with which to defend herself. She found a pair of scissors and some pins. As she began to place the items in her gown, she felt a hand come over her mouth.

She bit down hard and heard a man utter an oath.

He pulled her tightly up against him and whispered in her ear, "A spirited one. I am going to enjoy every minute of taming you."

She struggled against her captor with elbows and fists, but he did not fight fairly as her instruction had taught. She finally managed to pull forward enough to hike up her dress, and she kicked him as hard as she could where her brother once told her she could incapacitate a man if she struck hard enough.

Dannon let go and grabbed himself protectively as his face turned sallow. "You will pay for this!" He sneered at her while groaning in pain, unable to retaliate.

She kicked him again, and one more time for good measure.

"That is for all the other innocents, you blackguard!"

Hoping he would be incapacitated for a few minutes, she looked into the front room to see Yardley and Madame Clement still arguing. She was debating her options when Dannon grabbed her ankle. She was able to scream this time, and Yardley and Madame hurried to the doorway.

"Well, well, this is quaint," Madame Clement goaded. "We could have fun with her first," she taunted Yardley.

"Lillian, hush," Dannon groaned.

"Has she already had the best of you?" she chided.

"You really do not know when to desist, do you?" Jolie could take it no more and planted Madame a facer the Gentleman himself would be proud of.

Madame muttered an oath and held her hand to her bloodied nose.

Yardley was pulling on Jolie's arm to escape when she heard a gun cock. When a shot then sounded, they ran into the front room and to the door.

"Run, Jolie!" Yardley shouted.

She turned to see he was on the floor. Had he been hit? Jolie panicked. Leaving Yardley was not an option, and she could think of only one thing to do. She opened the door and whistled.

Dido came rushing to the door.

"Good girl," she whispered as she removed the gun he had strapped to the saddle. Madame Clement had reloaded and was aiming at Yardley again. Jolie prayed the gun she was holding was loaded, took aim, and fired.

Madame Clement fell to the ground and Jolie rushed to check on

Yardley.

"Are you hurt?"

He smiled at her looking dazed. "When did you learn to whistle?"

"Did she hurt you?" Jolie repeated.

He shook his head. "Just a scratch."

"Then why are you on the floor?"

He indicated an area that was bleeding on his arm. She found a scrap of fabric and bound the wound for him. He struggled to his feet, and seemed to come to his senses. "We have to deal with Dannon," he insisted.

She nodded her head and they walked back into the dressing room. Unsurprisingly, Dannon was not there.

Yardley leaned down to check to see if Lillian was still alive. When he was certain she was dead, he closed her eyes. He took the gun from Jolie and went to his horse, who was still standing in the doorway.

"Where is Madame Monique?" he asked. "I must go after Dannon. Can you stay here until the Runners arrive?"

She nodded. "I sent her to summon Mr Peters. They should be here any moment."

"Good girl." He picked up Lillian's gun and handed it to her before he kissed her and headed for the door.

"Dannon could not have gone too far on foot. I made sure of that," she called to him as he mounted the horse with a grimace.

He raised eyebrows at her comment, and blew her a kiss before riding away.

Jolie looked down at Madame Clement and began to shake and cry as the realisation of what she had done hit her. She wished she had not had to kill the woman, but she would do it again. It had been him or her.

Within a few minutes, Madame Monique arrived with the Runners.

"Yardley is out looking for Lord Dannon. Please help him," Jolie pleaded. "He is injured."

"I will find him," Peters reassured. "There were several men outside watching the area, and I am sure they are assisting him."

"I wish they had assisted earlier," she muttered.

"I will send someone to remove the body. But if you could wait here until I can speak to you."

Jolie nodded. "Just bring Yardley back to me safely."

As Benedict rode away from the *modiste's* shop, he tried to concentrate, but his head and arm were throbbing with pain. He must have hit his head when he fell down after being shot. Where were all the men who were supposed to be watching the shop? Would it be too much to hope they were chasing Dannon?

"If you were Dannon, where would you go?" he asked himself out loud.

He would probably head for the Channel. Did Dannon have a boat? Would he leave from the London docks, or from another port? London was too busy, as was Portsmouth. What was the closest departure point to Jersey? In all likelihood it was Weymouth, but he doubted Dannon would risk staying in the country long enough to travel there. Portsmouth was much more probable, but it was also busy and swarming with the military. He chose the southern road out of London and took the most direct route to the coast.

His head hurt, and he was seeing double of everything. He noticed people waving at him so he pulled the horse to a stop. It was one, not two, of Sir John's men.

"Your Grace?"

"Yes it is I. Did you see Lord Dannon leaving the *modiste's*?" He squinted at the man, trying to focus his eyes.

"I cannot say for sure who it was. But Dobson saw a man hobble out of the back door and followed him. He hailed a hackney cab and headed south. Dobson is following him."

"Excellent," Benedict said. "I am heading to the coast. Go back to the shop and make sure Lady Beaujolais is safe. When Peters arrives, let him know we are chasing Dannon. Send any man you can find to scour the docks here. There will be a generous reward for whomever finds him."

"Yes, your Grace."

Benedict urged his horse forward and onto the London Road.

As he rode, he tried to consider where Dannon could be. He was not as familiar with the south coast as he wished.

Benedict decided if he himself were being chased, he would seek the fastest route out. He took a chance and headed for it.

When he finally arrived at the coast his head was splitting and he felt dizzy, but he had to see this through. He decided to start with the nearest public house and ask. Benedict suspected he would be leaving with empty pockets in order to find the information he sought. Everyone knew these towns existed by smuggling, and they were extremely protective of their 'gentlemen'.

There were three taverns to choose from, and he selected the most inconspicuous of them all. It would be his choice if he were smuggling humans. That was a disturbing thought in itself.

"Good afternoon, m'lord," a rough-looking barkeeper said to him through rotten teeth.

Benedict suspected he did not look himself at the moment as there had been no time to change his attire, but his fine clothing and boots indicated a gentleman of means.

"I am looking for a man who goes by the name of Dannon," Benedict said.

"I ain't heard of 'im," the barkeeper said, though his eyes were shifty.

Benedict laid several crowns upon the bar, but kept his hand hovering over them. "Is your memory refreshed?"

"Mayhap I heard of him," the barkeeper replied and looked smug as he took the crowns.

"If you lead me to him, there will be a handsome reward. However, if I find out you are abetting him, I will personally oversee the building of your gallows."

"He came through here not half an hour past. He keeps a boat down by the cave. That is all I know, I swear it."

"How do I get to the cave?" Benedict demanded.

The man looked reluctant to give any more information. Benedict pulled him up by his collar.

"You and t'other lordly fellow are mighty rough."

"What other lordly fellow?"

"The one wit' one arm and one eye." The barkeeper shuddered in recollection.

Fairmont. Fairmont was here! Benedict was hopeful.

"Ye'll never find it on yer own."

"Then find someone to guide me. If I find out you are in any way involved with the girls he has kidnapped, you will not make it as far as the gallows," Benedict threatened.

Sweat beaded on the barkeeper's brow.

"If you have anything to tell me, you had best say it now."

"I don't know nothin' 'bout no kidnapped girls. I told t'other flash cove. T'one ye call Dannon is known to help sell some of t'goods and bring back a few things in return."

"Very well. Take me to the cave."

It was a surprisingly steep and long walk down to the shore. Benedict stumbled and lost his footing several times.

"What is inside?" he asked, when they reached the mouth of the cave.

"I don't know nothin' 'bout what's inside."

"When is the next boat scheduled to come in?"

"It goes by the moon. 'Tis 'bout time for one. It has been 'bout a fortnight since t'last."

Benedict was losing patience. He knew this man was feigning innocence. He wanted to find Fairmont, and possibly Hughes, to see what they had discovered. It was likely they had more information than he did.

"Where are the boats kept?" he asked as he looked around with no boats in sight.

"Far away from the revenue man."

"Very well. You may return to your post. If your information helps I will see you get your reward."

The man touched his hat and scurried away.

Benedict still had time before it grew dark. He looked about and wondered if Dannon could see him. There was little to see other than the water and the rocks surrounding the cave and cliffs. He wondered where Fairmont and Hughes could be. Should he explore the cave?

He decided that would be foolhardy when he was injured and no one knew where he was. He instead found a large boulder to hide behind, and rested his eyes while he waited for darkness.

He was aroused from slumber some time later. He was disorientated and it took time to recall his whereabouts, but the smell of the sea air and the sounds of waves lapping the shore quickly brought him back to reality. He felt as though a hammer was pounding on his head and it was difficult to see anything clearly. He heard voices echo, which must be coming from the cave less than thirty feet from his hiding spot. He perched down lower and tried to focus. He was not feeling terribly confident in the dark on his own. He desperately hoped Hughes and Fairmont had a plan, and some men to support it.

When it finally came into view, the smuggling boat was anchored out in the harbour and smaller rowing boats were being deployed to come to the shore.

Throughout his life, Benedict had heard tales about smugglers and their nefarious business, but he had never witnessed it. It was rather more fascinating and complex than his young mind had dreamt when he'd been a boy. The oarsmen rowed stealthily in a unified fashion, and they were met quietly by others from the caves to unload. Benedict's interest was piqued when they began to bring out supplies to send back on the boat. Several barrels and crates were rolled from inside. He could see no one resembling Dannon, and certainly no-one small enough to be young girls.

He was trying to be patient, but how much longer could he wait? He could not take all of these men on alone, and he had no indication that they knew about the girls.

"Hughes and Fairmont, where are you?" he whispered. He should have asked when the barkeeper last saw them. Perhaps they had given up and gone elsewhere.

The men were beginning to disperse from the cave. There was no possibility he could defend himself against so many, should they choose to attack him. He still had no indication that any of the persons involved were even here. The smugglers stowed their goods and then left. Benedict gave up, and had begun walking away when he heard shots fired from the boat. He took off into the water, wincing as he stepped on the pebbled beach. It was not long before he heard others scrambling down the path again. The smugglers must have heard the shots as well. He only hoped he was not too late, and that the girls, Fairmont, and Hughes, were unharmed if they were involved as he suspected.

When Benedict finally reached the smugglers' boat, he heard mayhem and shouting in French.

He yelled to them in their language to throw down the ladder.

"Non!" was the reply received.

"I am a duke, not an excise man! I want to help the person who was shot!" he insisted in their native tongue.

After some discussion amongst themselves, they tossed the ladder to him. Although exhausted, he heaved himself over the side.

The men were all speaking rapidly in a dialect he could scarcely understand. He held up his hands and asked for only one person to speak.

"*Rapidement*! We must sail quickly before we are captured," the Captain said anxiously.

"What has happened?"

"*Meutre!*"

"Murder? Who was murdered?"

"*Monsieur.*"

"Where is he?"

"*Bas.*"

"Take me to him. *S'il vous plaît.*"

The man looked terrified and told his men to prepare to set sail. As they began to climb into the hold, the sound of barrels being prised opened could be heard.

The Captain began yelling for them to stop, but when Benedict made it down the steps, he discovered Fairmont and Hughes were helping the missing girls climb out of the wine barrels that had just been brought on board.

He hurried to assist before looking over and seeing Dannon's dead body cast off to the side. He nudged the corpse with his foot to satisfy himself.

"About time, Yardley," Fairmont drawled.

"I have been waiting on shore for hours, thank you very much."

"Let us get these girls to safety, then we can share our grievances over a tankard or two," Fairmont suggested.

"What do you mean to do with Dannon?" Benedict asked.

"The French can throw him overboard, for all I care." Fairmont spat on the dead body for emphasis.

"If we do not hurry, we will be sailing to France ourselves," Hughes said.

"God forbid," he muttered.

They assisted the girls into a small rowing boat, which Benedict had to pay the French captain a small fortune for, then Hughes helped him row them back to the shore. He was uncertain how he had managed the feat while concussed and exhausted, once he reached the shore. Shortly after they had pulled away from the larger boat, they heard Dannon being fed to the fish with a loud splash as soon as the Frenchmen sailed away. Dannon's body would wash ashore sooner or later, long after they were gone.

The girls were huddled in the small boat, and none said a word. Benedict did not feel much like speaking either, and he had not been through a fraction of what they must have endured.

Peters was waiting for them when they reached the shore, and they handed the girls over and hired a carriage to take them back to London.

Chapter Twenty-two

After two hours of waiting, judging by the plain timepiece behind the counter, Jolie's father arrived at the dressmaker's shop. It had been arranged that they would return to Ashbury House by tea, and if they did not, he was to come hotfoot. In his wake followed two burly footmen, armed with heavy clubs. Madame Monique had returned, but she had promptly had a fit of hysterics and had retired to her rooms with her vinaigrette. Jolie was so relieved to see a familiar face in her father after looking at Madame Clement's dead body, killed by her own hand.

The woman's face would haunt her for the rest of her life.

They had returned home, and she had paced the parlour for hours after having a bath, with no word from the Runners. Her mother had finally coaxed her into retiring with the promise to wake her should there be word. She now lay in her bed trying to forget about the day, but it still was not over. She had heard nothing from Yardley, and she could not help but fear the worst.

She had done little to tell him her true feelings. She regretted so many things; how she had behaved towards him, what she had said, and the way she said it. She doubted not that he knew she cared for him, but he did not know the depth of her feelings. She wanted to change that if she ever saw him again.

She threw her covers back, rose from her bed and paced the floor. How could she be expected to sleep when he could be stranded somewhere, needing her?

She decided she had to at least try to help. She began to dress herself, and as she was rummaging through her drawers, there was a knock on the door and her mother stepped inside.

"What are you doing, dearest? It is four in the morning. I understand you cannot sleep. However, you cannot go anywhere at this hour."

"But he is out there alone!" she protested.

"He is not alone, Jolie. The Runners are helping."

Her mother led her to a chair and sat next to her. "I am certain. Your father spoke to Sir John a little while ago," she said calmly.

"What if something has happened to him? I have not told him how I feel, *Maman.*"

"I do think you should tell him, and perhaps show him, too, when next you see him."

She reached over and pulled the bell-rope, and when the servant arrived, yawning none-too-discreetly, sent for a cordial to help Jolie sleep.

"I cannot sleep," Jolie insisted. "I want to know when he arrives."

"I promise to wake you. I promise." Her mother handed her the cordial to drink before she kissed her on the forehead and left after she had put her back to bed.

It was still several hours before they had word. Jolie was awake and dressed, and was more anxious than ever.

There was only one thing that would ease her mind. She sought out the pianoforte in the music room. Her fingers automatically began to play the song her heart sang whenever she thought of him. If only she could speak to him through music, he would understand he was her everything. She could imagine him next to her, as she recalled that special night with him at Yardley. They had both been themselves, without any pretence. She could take back none of the words she had already spoken, but she would try to express her feelings for him in a better way.

"And I know that he loves me," she said aloud. "But he needs to know that I love him," she continued, as a tear rolled down her cheek. "I never told him."

"He knows."

His arms came around her and his hands joined hers on the keys. She was encompassed by his warmth and his scent, and she knew within his arms was where she belonged. Her hands could no longer play the melody in her heart at that moment, for she needed his touch. She turned to face him as he joined her on the bench and stroked her cheek. His tawny eyes reflected all the love and tenderness she felt as his lips came over hers and expressed what words could not. Emotion overcame her, and she broke down in tears. Benedict's arms surrounded her once more and held her for some time.

"Benedict, I do not wish to wait."

"I do not either, my love, but there will be scandal."

"Of course there will. I had not considered you might not wish to be married to a murderess."

"This entire affair has been horrid; two evil people ruining countless lives. I wish I could say they can no longer hurt anyone, but I know it is not true. Their legacy will haunt all of the innocent victims they have harmed from beyond the grave."

"It will certainly affect me always," Jolie said.

"I, too, still have nightmares about the duel over Lillian which ended a man's life. The pain never completely goes away, but it does hurt less as time passes."

"When I think of everything she did, I am not sorry she is dead; I daresay only that I killed her."

"I understand."

"I want to know what happened. The girls are safe?"

"I will start from the beginning. I was rather disorientated when I left the shop. Thankfully, I was stopped by one of the runners, who told me they were following Dannon. I decided to go where I would choose if I were trying to escape. It was a fortunate guess. I found a barkeeper—whom I had to pay and threaten—in order to find out where Dannon's operation was. It was the night for a smuggling ship to come in, so I found a place to hide near the cave."

Jolie gasped. "That was dangerous!"

"Wait a moment before you have visions of my heroism. I watched, but did not see any girls or Dannon. There were so many men, I did nothing. It was not until the goods had been exchanged, and the smugglers had left the beach, that I came out of my hiding place."

Jolie laughed at his self-deprecating expression.

"It was only after I began to walk away, that I heard gunshots. I immediately swam to the boat and the French Captain allowed me to come aboard. It was mayhem, and their dialect was difficult for me to understand. However, 'murder' and 'Monsieur' caught my attention."

"What happened? The suspense is more than I can bear!" Jolie exclaimed.

"When we went down below to the hold, there were Hughes and Fairmont helping the girls. They had been stowed away in wine barrels."

"How did they come to be on board?"

"You have seen Lord Fairmont. I am certain there was bribery in addition to some physical convincing."

"So where had the shots come from?"

"Fairmont shot Dannon."

"Dannon is dead also?" she asked in disbelief, her eyes wide.

"He looked quite dead and was thrown into the sea as soon as we made our exit."

"That death was too kind for him," Jolie said with disgust.

"I doubt Fairmont let him die without any suffering."

"I can only imagine what he would have done to me," she said with a shudder of disgust.

"I would rather not," he snapped. "I think it fitting that Fairmont was the one to rid the earth of his filth. Perhaps Lady Fairmont will have some peace now."

"Let us pray it is so."

"I still do not understand why they were forced to return to England," she said, perplexed.

"Ah, yes. My mother was able to discover the missing link on her shopping expedition."

"Very clever of her," Jolie laughed.

"While we were fending off Lillian and Dannon, she walked into each shop and offered a reward for anyone who could tell her anything about Lord Dannon or Madame Clement."

"And what did she discover?"

"Lillian and Dannon had been cast out of France when they were discovered to be kidnapping young girls. Monsieur Clement was the one who turned them in."

"So they killed him?"

"I cannot answer with certainty. The young girl Mother discovered only worked in the shops in Paris. However, Clement's accounts were swept clean, and a generous donation was made to gain our Prince Regent's favour, and entrée into England."

Jolie was still attempting to sort out everything in her mind.

"How did Fairmont and Hughes come to be on the boat?"

"They had travelled to Jersey, and discovered that Dannon had not yet arrived. They followed the same logic and tactics that I did. Fairmont was able to bribe the Frenchman, and he stowed away until Dannon and the girls arrived."

"I am thankful you did not have to face him alone."

"I would have been too late," he said gravely.

"Where were all of the Runners?"

"Some were searching the London docks, some went to Paris, some to Jersey, and there were some onshore waiting for us. It was too risky for them to take extra people onboard the small boat."

"What do you think will happen to me?" she asked.

"There will be an inquest, of course. But you saved my life, Jolie. Between your father and me, we hope to prevent you from having to testify. We have Madame Monique to support our claims, though no one is going to doubt what truly happened."

"Then we can be married? That is, if you can handle the scandal," she added with a mischievous smile.

"What is one more to me?" he said drily.

"Would you mind terribly if we forgo a large wedding? I know my mother will be disappointed; however, I do not have the heart for it. All that matters to me is to be with you."

"All that matters to me is your happiness," he said, as he bent his head and brushed his mouth across hers. He pulled back and met her look of pleasure with a loving smile. Then, taking her face in both hands, he claimed her lips again in a tender kiss that expressed all of the emotions she was feeling: relief, happiness, sadness, fear, passion and love. She had not known a kiss could be so intimate and consuming.

"I could get used to this," Benedict murmured when the kiss finally ended. He took her hands in his and brushed his thumb over the top of hers. Jolie remained with her eyes closed, and with a smile that would last for days.

"Unfortunately, my love, there is unfinished business. I must return to Jersey with Fairmont and Hughes, to release the other girls we believe Dannon is holding there against their will. Fairmont is speaking with His Majesty at this moment, in order to gain his support should we have trouble with the authorities in Jersey."

"I would like to come with you." She held up her hand before he could protest. "Hear me out. Do you not think the girls will be afraid of more men? It would be better for them if I go with you. Perhaps Lady Fairmont would also be willing."

He smiled lovingly at her. "Lady Fairmont thought the same. I would be pleased to have you by my side," he said.

"I am most encouraged to know you may be reasoned with," she said with an impudent grin.

"I was not expecting so much impertinence before the wedding," he replied with mock hauteur.

"You are fortunate indeed," she bantered.

He silenced her with a kiss that left her speechless until the Fairmonts arrived to leave for Jersey.

Epilogue

Jolie felt the first hints of the sun on her face and the fresh breeze of the sea air wafting through the open balcony doors. She stretched her arms and felt the warmth of her husband next to her. She smiled and studied him while he slept.

She had been utterly mistaken about him, and she was ever so thankful she had been given the opportunity to be proven wrong. She ran her finger down his chest, through the dusting of light hair, and he twitched. Not wishing to disturb him, but no longer able to sleep, she rose from the bed and walked out onto the balcony as she felt a small kick from the new life growing inside her. She smiled as she relished the thought of having Benedict's child living within her, and knew they would deservedly have a mischievous child.

It had been months since their wedding, but Jolie had at last persuaded Benedict to take a holiday in France. She was determined to erase his ill opinion of the country of her youth and show him the delights of being married to a French woman.

They had married by Special Licence quietly in front of their closest friends and family in the gardens at Ashbury Court, surrounded by the birds and fragrant blooms of summer.

Between them, her mother and Madame Monique had insisted on creating an exquisite gown of lavender silk, overlaid with ivory lace and pearl trim, coming together with a diamond brooch over the bodice. The Ashbury tiara of pearls and diamonds decorated her ebony locks, while crystal-studded slippers fit for a duchess adorned her feet. Her mother had been disappointed there was to be no grandiose *ton* wedding, Jolie had finally agreed to that lady throwing a ball upon their return.

The only persons missing were Anjou and Charles. It was hard not to wish her siblings had been with her, but word had been received her brother and sister had arrived safely in Virginia, at last. The girls who had been rescued from Dannon's brothel in Jersey—there were twelve more found—had worked tirelessly to help with her gown and other wedding preparations, which had made it all the more perfect. Jolie could not have enjoyed the wedding completely had the girls not been safe. Jemima returned to Madame Monique, and the others went to the Easton's school until they were prepared to go back into the world.

Jolie sighed with contentment as she stole another glance at Benedict. By the smile he wore in his sleep, she must be doing a fair job of representing France. She leaned on the balustrade to watch the sun rise over the blue hues of the Mediterranean. There were a few small fishing vessels, but the only sounds came from the gulls overhead and the waves crashing on the cliffs below. She would love to capture this moment in time. She had never been happier, and she knew it would not last forever.

She felt a strong arm slip around her and pull her close against his warm chest. *"Bonjour, ma coeur,"* he whispered into her ear, sending shivers down her spine. He kissed her neck, but then placed his chin on her shoulder and joined her. Her gaze became misty as they both stared out over the ocean.

"Do you know, husband mine, I believe our *Pride and Prejudice* authoress is wrong."

"How so, my sweet?" he murmured, without lifting his gaze from the dulcet scene before them.

"'Happiness in marriage is entirely a matter of *choice*, not *chance*!'"

He chuckled, a warm, throaty sound, which told her he would not be content to stare at the ocean for long.

Jolie cherished these moments as much as the more passionate ones, for they needed the counterpoint in their relationship. He seemed to need the quieter, more tender moments more than she would have ever supposed.

In all likelihood, he would still be cold and pompous to those who knew him not, but to her, he would be her warm, loving Duke.

Thank you for reading *Melting the Ice*. I hope you enjoyed it. If you did, please help other readers find this book:

1. Share the book with a friend who you think might like it so she or he can discover me, too.
2. Help other people find this book by writing a review.
3. Sign up for my new releases at www.Elizabethjohnsauthor.com, so you can find out about the next book as soon as it's available.
4. Come like my Facebook page www.facebook.com/Elizabethjohnsauthor or follow on Twitter @Ejohnsauthor or write me at elizabethjohnsauthor@gmail.com

Other Titles by Elizabeth Johns:

Surrender the Past

Seasons of Change

Seeking Redemption

Shadows of Doubt

Second Dance

Through the Fire

First Impressions

About the Author

Like many writers, Elizabeth Johns was first an avid reader, though she was a reluctant convert. It was Jane Austen's clever wit and unique turn of phrase that hooked Johns when she was 'forced' to read Pride and Prejudice for a school assignment. She began writing when she ran out of her favourite author's books and decided to try her hand at crafting a Regency romance novel. Her journey into publishing began with the release of Surrender the Past, book one of the Loring-Abbott Series. Johns makes no pretensions to Austen's wit, but hopes readers will perhaps laugh and find some enjoyment in her writing.

Johns attributes much of her inspiration to her mother, a former English teacher. During their last summer together, Johns would sit on the porch swing and read her stories to her mother, who encouraged her to continue writing. Busy with multiple careers, including a professional job in the medical field, writing and mother of small children, Johns squeezes in time for reading whenever possible.

Preview of With the Wind

"*Maman, Papa,*" Anjou said to her parents when she found them alone together in the drawing room. She had finally worked up the courage to speak to them about something she had at last resolved to do.

"What is it, Anjou?" her father asked.

"I need to go to America," she blurted out.

Her parents exchanged a look.

"I still have investigators looking for Aidan, dear. It is not safe to let you go to America alone," her father tried to reason with her.

"But for how much longer, *Papa*?" she asked, making no effort to mask her frustration.

"Until you are satisfied he is no longer alive," he answered with a frown.

"Charles has agreed to go with me." She stood as she argued her case.

"Has he?" her father said with an arch look. "I wonder that he did not think to consult with me first."

"*Papa,*" she said quietly, "Do not be cross with Charles. I am not brave enough to go alone, and I asked him to accompany me before I came to you. I must do this. I do not *want* to do this, but I must."

"Why we ever agreed to let you and Aidan do this, I cannot remember," her mother said with regret

"*Maman,* you love Aidan as much as I. I know there is but a small chance I will find him alive, but it needs to be done. I cannot go on with my life until I know for certain."

"Where do you mean to stay? How do you mean to get there? Have you thought of the realities of travelling across an ocean to an unknown

226

land?" her father objected rather harshly.

"Charles has a friend who captains a ship back and forth on a regular basis. He is going to take us to Virginia to the Eastons' plantation. I had hoped to make contact with your investigators to see what they have discovered, and where they have already looked for him." She continued to press her case as her parents listened to her well-considered reasoning. "I thought, perhaps, if he looks different, or is injured somewhere, I might be able to recognise him when they cannot."

"You have been thinking of this a great deal," her father remarked .

"I have thought of little else for four years," she said quietly. "I have tried to consider him as dead and think of other suitors, but I cannot."

Her mother put her hands to her head and shook it back and forth. "I do not want you to go. Can Charles not go alone? He was his best friend— he could certainly recognise him."

"But I am his wife."

"No one else knows, Anjou," her mother protested.

Her father let out a sigh. "An error in judgement I continue to regret. You do not require our permission to go."

"I would prefer to have it, just the same."

Her father paused for some time, and she thought he would refuse. At last he gave a reluctant nod.

~*~

Anjou was terrified. She had never before crossed an ocean. She was not brave like her sisters, but she could not carry on with her life until she was certain. Her mind told her that Aidan could not be alive after four years, but her heart knew she must search for him. She had never sailed further than across the Channel from France to England, and she did not want to be on a boat now any more than she had then. If her brother Charles had not agreed to accompany her, she would have turned back by now.

She stood on the dock, watching as cargo was loaded onto the ship. The Isle of Wight, a short journey away, caused her to consider the distance she was about to travel with deepening dismay. The air was thick and hot, and the only relief from the smells of rotten fish and salty water was an occasional breeze. She prayed it would not smell so strongly the entire journey. Charles had told her there would be no other women aboard, save herself and her maid, so she feared the worst in that regard.

"Can I help you, miss?" asked a man in the deep voice of a gentleman. Anjou was startled, as she was lost in thought.

"I beg your pardon. I did not mean to frighten you, but a lady should not be left alone on the docks."

She looked upward to see an uncomfortably large man towering over her. He was sun-weathered, with several days' beard, but she could not make out his eyes for the sun's glare and the shadow of his hat.

"I am not alone. I am with my brother and my maid. He was searching for someone to load our trunks," she replied, feeling unaccountably comfortable around this stranger, to whom she had not been introduced.

"Onto the *Wind*?" he asked doubtfully.

"Is that the name of this ship?" she asked, for some odd reason forgetting his question and smiling.

"Her full name is *With the Wind*, but we call her *Wind* for short." His eyes twinkled with amusement.

"It was meant to be, then," she said, as she looked at the large wooden vessel with tall poles and sails and ropes, which was somehow supposed to remain upright on the ocean. She resolved to be less afraid if this was her destiny.

"What was meant to be?" he asked suspiciously.

"My trip to America." She considered him more closely, wondering why it would matter to him. His eyes were a strange colour of greyish-green, and were very disconcerting when they were examining her from head to toe.

"Might I be so bold as to ask who your brother is?"

"Charles Winslow. He is a friend of the Captain."

"He is, is he?"

"Are you going to introduce yourself, then?" she asked, growing impatient with his questions.

"Edward Harris, at your service." He removed his hat and proffered an elegant bow. He replaced his hat on his head and continued, "Captain of the *Wind*."

"I am…"

He interrupted. "I know exactly who you are my lady, and I am not at all happy about it."

Acknowledgements

There are many, many people who have contributed to making my books possible.

My family, who deals with the idiosyncrasies of a writer's life that do not fit into a 9 to 5 work day.

Dad, who reads every single version before and after anyone else—that alone qualifies him for sainthood.

Wilette, who takes my visions and interprets them, making them into works of art people want to read.

Karen, Tina, Staci, Judy, Shae and Kristiann who care about my stories enough to help me shape them before everyone else sees them.

Tessa and Heather who help me say what I mean to, and make the process more fun.

I am forever grateful to you all.

Made in United States
North Haven, CT
27 August 2022

23365388R00139